PEGGY PINCH, POLICEMAN'S WIFE

As a young man, Malcolm Noble served in the Hampshire Police, a chapter in his life that provides some background to his crime fiction. He has written nine mystery novels set in the south of England from the 1920s through to the 1960s. Press reviews have emphasised the author's sense of place and atmosphere, his strong characterisation and first rate storytelling.

Malcolm Noble lives in Market Harborough where he and his wife run a bookshop.

Peggy Pinch

Pinch

Policeman's Wife

Best Wishes
Malc Noble

Malcolm Noble

Matador
5 Weir Road
Kibworth Beauchamp
Leicester LE8 0LQ, UK
Tel: (+44) 116 279 2299
Fax: (+44) 116 279 2277
Email: books@troubador.co.uk
Web: www.troubador.co.uk/matador

This is a work of fiction. All characters and events are imaginary
and any resemblance to actual characters and events is purely coincidental.

ISBN 978 1848767 867

British Library Cataloguing in Publication Data.
A catalogue record for this book is available from the British Library.

Typeset in 10.5pt Stempel Garamond by Troubador Publishing Ltd, Leicester, UK

Matador is an imprint of Troubador Publishing Ltd

Printed in Great Britain by the MPG Books Group, Bodmin and King's Lynn

To Christine

PART ONE

CHAPTER ONE

Peggity Pinch, the policeman's wife, put a raincoat over her nightdress and stepped out to check on the schoolma'am's cat. PC Pinch was working late and Peggy, unable to settle until he was indoors, had put up with the cat's screeching and scratching for more than an hour. Queen O'Scots was being a nuisance – no more, no less – but Peggy couldn't get rid of a worry that the pet had caught herself in the chicken-wire that Pinch had recently threaded through their front hedge.

She got to the gate as Miss Carstairs threw open a bedroom window, opposite. "Is she being wicked, the spoilt madam?"

"She's fine," Peggy called. "She's run off into the night. She'll come to no harm, not round here."

Seven miles away, Tom Hall was running hard. Sticks and stalks bit at his ankles. Wet from the trees got into the collar and sleeves of his poacher's jacket. The air was so cold that it turned crispy on his eyebrows and the tufts of ginger bum-fluff that grew on an inch of purple cheek, each side of his nose. It was five minutes to midnight; treacherous moonlight broke through the trees above him, throwing phoney colours across his muddied face, and the sounds of his thrashing and tumbling lifted through the branches and broke free into the night. He wanted to wipe a hand across his forehead but he was too good at the game to do that; he knew he would drag grit and sweat into his eyes. His lungs were wretched, blood ached in his left shoulder and he knew that an old gouge to his hip would force him down in the end. But Tom bent his back and kept going. He was winning.

The horseman was away to his left, covering the rough meadow that sloped down to the railway line. The rider hoped to run Tom down when he broke from the coppice. Tom pictured the familiar expression on old Corquet's face – the pursed thin lips, the nostrils that flexed almost imperceptibly as they took in breath. And the hard fixed eyes that never let you go. 'The devil's pig-sticker,' thought Tom. He knew that the old cavalry officer would be coaxing him, under his breath – 'Come round, come round,' like a whipper-in willing a wayward stag to a trap. He'd want Tom to make a race of it so that they would come to grips at Holt's Crossing in the bed of the valley. Major Corquet was a good horseman and a fine shot – but Tom Hall was just as clever.

Tom hadn't been shy of making a noise; he wanted the Major to think that he was reckless. But, at the edge of the wood, Tom dropped into a ditch, just six paces short of the front line of cover, and ferreted until he had a view through the twigs and long grass. (He had been taught to look through cover, never over its top.) It was a grey night with the charcoal shapes and shadows that spectres were made of. Every noise – every crack, every knock – had the hollowness of a child's echo calling for its mother. Suddenly, a nighthawk beat up the field, not six feet off the ground. It swerved and dipped, then rose to a stall before sweeping down, its further flight obscured by a thicket that intruded from the parish boundary. 'She'll have caught her prey,' Tom thought. 'She didn't look like a bird who'd lose.' Then there was quiet. Frail clouds moved away from the moon and, for the next few minutes, everything was clear. Down at the crossing, the Major's erect figure on horseback was unmistakable but Tom also spied an unknown figure, standing in the lee of two lineside huts.

Tom had been taught to judge the height and weight of an observed subject; he also fancied he could get the target's age within five years. The figure was four-fifths of the height of the eaves of the hut and moved his shoulders and arms like a ten stone man. (Careful, Private Hall, be sure to correct for the bias of a sniper lying down.) The mystery stalker was not nervous, but impish; he would rather lean back than duck down. Tom guessed that he wouldn't be more

4

than twenty-five, and could be younger. The distance and the night meant that Tom couldn't make out any personal features, but he was sure this was a man he hadn't seen before.

Tom wanted to laugh out loud. How fickle it all was! Ten years ago, a fit Private Hall had been Corquet's scout in some forsaken farmlands behind enemy lines. The Major had been quick to recognise the fieldcraft of this ne'er-do-well from his home village. He had taken him out of the trenches, blessed his skills with the wisdom of warfare and then called him 'my man'. Sometimes Tom 'reccied' for only an hour at night but there had been times when he endured two and three days before he could get back. Days spent scavenging, napping, crawling on his belly with his insides parched dry and knitted with fear. He grew certain that his superior meant to send him on mission after mission until he failed to return. One evening, when they were drinking alone in a shell-shot schoolhouse, Tom had asked the question directly, and got a curt dismissal: "What is one life, my man, weighed against the thousands we're losing in the trenches?" At least, thought Tom, a spy on his own has some control over his destiny. "Don't worry," laughed the Major. "We are both smart enough to survive and go home."

Home, to this. As Tom watched the village squire on horseback, crossing from one side of the railway track to the other, he recognised that 'Old Corker' had always been his enemy. 'Corker' was the bad man who had taken him into ownership and exploited him, sending him into danger and, each time, setting the fences higher. He deserved a bullet.

Tom's hatred for Eustace Corquet had been chiselled in stone on a cold night at Verdun, when three chums shared a Woodbine. They spoke in whispers, not because of a need for secrecy but because the harshness of the air made them keep their breath shallow. Tom heard about a poor baker's youth from Staffordshire, who had lied about his age and pretended to be brave but, turned stupid by months in the trenches, stood up straight one morning and called for Fritz to shoot him. He went on calling until, in the cruellest joke of this simpleton's war, a gun had fired from his own side. Tom had always blamed Corquet for the lad's death because, even if this pompous toff hadn't been near the trenches that night, the bullet had come from one of his ilk. That's the right and wrong of it, never mind the truth.

Now, for two pins, he would have stood on the top of Holt's Ridge and waved his arms like that madman. But it was better to keep the Major guessing.

Yes, Corquet was curious. He had expected Tom to make a barefaced run for it but now he suspected a more complicated game. What was the scoundrel up to? He patted the horse's shoulder and asked the question aloud. Then he slowly wheeled around, surveying the panorama of darkened countryside. He knew no man who could run through the night better than Tom Hall. Perhaps the 'Flanders Fox' had already slipped away, or was he waiting for Corquet to give up the advantage of the crossing? Now, instead of being ahead of the game, the Major felt somehow tethered to the railway tracks. His thoroughbred sensed the uncertainty and began to show some restlessness.

Tom, enjoying the Major's indecision, edged himself to the brow of the ditch. He was sure that time was on his side. The Major would know that he was being watched and wouldn't be able to put up with it; he would move on. Tom chuckled, "Remember the rules, Corkers. When suspicious, watch. When watching, learn."

Tom had the benefit of high ground and, in the good moonlight, could make out most of what was going on. As the chestnut mare and her rider started to wander along the track, the mystery character at the lineside huts moved to keep out of the Major's sight. Then Tom heard someone move in the thicket to his right, half-way down the hill. Tom was ready to give more attention to that trespasser, when he noticed that the horse had stopped. Her head was up. Something had alerted her.

At first, the noise was a low rumble in the trees to the left of the stage. Then, as it grew nearer, Tom identified the rattling and clanking of a double-headed freight train emerging from the woods. That was unusual. The days had gone when this single branch line was busy at night and there was usually no work for the heavy locomotives from an industrial region but here, two of the local 'black motors' had been called up to haul a long train. It progressed across the scene, unannounced and unhurried and making no stutter. He counted twelve, twenty, more than thirty flatbed trucks loaded with military equipment. Vans, cannon, tractors and armoured cars. Each wagon was lit with two lanterns and carried a man with a rifle.

Tom thought, this wasn't an everyday movement of ordnance. The local army camps weren't served by the branch line and couldn't have accommodated a shipment of this size. Perhaps the Major had heard about the cargo and had ridden out to observe its passage through his neighbourhood (reducing his encounter with Tom to no more than a playful sideshow).

Then, when the tail of the train was drawing away, a gunshot cracked across the night sky. Birds squawked high in the air. The mare reared up. The Major cried out and dropped to the ground.

Tom ducked down in the dirt and didn't lift his head until he was sure that no alarm had been raised. Hardly moving, hardly breathing, Tom peered through the undergrowth and tried to make sense of things. The Major's body hadn't moved and the horse stood over it, quietly, steadfastly, patiently obedient. The middle thicket was quiet, the lineside huts were still and, although the train could be heard, its sound was now more than a mile away. Tom heard a fox prowling along the rough hedge that led to Thurrock's Farm and he smiled to himself; four men were on the scene – Tom, the clumsy trespasser in the thicket, the man at the lineside huts and the dead Major – yet the fox was so little threatened by them that he continued to tread through the night. Then Tom saw a fifth figure running in from the greyness. A man who wasn't built for running but whose fear put extra stamina in his legs. He was loose-footed. Stumbling, tripping. Slipping to either side as he crossed the troughs of the meadow. Twice, he had to reach down or he would have fallen. A big coat flapped about him and he carried a leather forage hat in his hands. He was running so blindly that he didn't see Tom and became aware of the ditch too late to save himself. With a gasp, he fell across Tom's legs. Tom rolled on top, twisting the youth's arms behind his back and covering his face with a hand.

"Boy Berkeley, I'll not hurt you, so you stay silent." After a few seconds, Tom relaxed his grip so that the youth could nod, then he took his hand away.

"Mr Halls, sir," he whispered urgently. His eyes were white and scared and his face was swollen, as if he had been stung by some sort of venom. "I didn't kill him."

"I know that, Boy. Neither did I. But we've both got to get away from here."

"Don't tell anyone I was hereabouts," he pleaded.

"And you keep your own mouth shut about it." But Tom knew that Boy Berkeley was so young for his age that he'd see no harm in telling half the folk in their village, one by one.

"No, no, Mr Halls. I won't blub."

He was a lad that Tom had been quick to ridicule, over the years, about his clumsiness and his slow uptake, but Tom knew that teasing was no good now; he had to scare the lad.

"The gun was fired from a military train, Boy, so do you think that the Major was killed by the government?"

"An execution?"

"And what do you think the government would do to anyone known to be here, tonight?"

"He was shot for being a spy? Do you think that, Mr Halls?"

Tom didn't dispute the idea. "And the rest of us?" he persisted.

"Likely, they'll come in the night and slit our throats in our beds and burn our houses down and all the good souls in it."

"Your mother?"

"I'll pray that she'll be saved."

"And your father?"

"I'd not care about him going to his maker."

"But you need to keep quiet."

Berkeley nodded. "Like a sworn oath, buttered in blood." But he wanted to be sure of Tom's side of the bargain. "You'll not tell on me, Mr Halls. You'll not split that I was out of our house at night."

Tom promised he never would.

He had always thought that Berkeley's face was odd. Now, as he studied it closely, desperate for any clue of what was truly going on

8

in the boy's muddled mind, Tom saw that the side of the head was banana-shaped; it must have been pushed about at birth. Berkeley had a good black growth on his cheeks, for a youth, and the alert eyes of the savage. 'You'll not make a soldier,' Tom thought, 'because you could never trust yourself to do as you're told, but you've a good face for a fighter.'

Berkeley had lived all his life, with just his mother and father, in a terraced cottage at the bottom of The Street. No-one saw much of the woman, other than evenings in church, and no-one went to their house. Every morning old Mr Berkeley had to be one of the first about because he delivered pots from a horse-drawn cart to each house in the village but Boy Berkeley had never done a day's work and people said he'd be in prison soon if he didn't wake up.

Tom asked: "Now, what were you up to, Boy Berkeley?"

"Getting about," said the lad. "It's the time to do it at night when no-one's about to give you instructions or make up stories about you." Then he asked plainly, "What are you doing in the woods, Mr Halls?"

"Baiting the bear," muttered Tom, sure that the youth didn't have the wit to make anything of the reply.

But Boy Berkeley understood much more. "You left Thin Jessie's house two hours ago and I think you were crossing country from Thurrock's farm. I don't know what for, except for business that needed doing before daylight."

Tom grabbed the lad's shoulder, forcing his thumb into the young muscle until the boy blinked like a Billy Bunter and his body curled into one side. "You keep quiet, Berkeley!"

"Of course, Mr Halls. Haven't I promised? I was just letting you know."

"Letting me know what?"

"That you need to keep quiet too, Mr Halls. It's only fair."

Tom pushed him back down in the ditch. "You be very sure what you're about before you start bad mouthing me."

The boy was close to tears now. "There was a man. You must have seen him as plainly as I did. That man, standing by the shed before the train went past."

9

"Who was it?"

Berkeley shook his head. "I couldn't make him out but you did see him, didn't you, Mr Halls?"

Tom said ponderously, "Yes, Ernest," using the Christian name for the first time. "Yes, I saw him."

"Who d'you think it was, Mr Halls?"

"Don't know, lad. But I can tell you that he was left handed."

"You can't have seen that, not from up here," Berkeley argued.

"When a man takes aim from cover, he'll look from his firing side. He doesn't need to be taught that way. It's natural. It's a man's way of giving himself the best protection. Mark my words, young Berkeley, that man at the lineside hut fires with his left hand."

"You learned that in the army?"

"Didn't need to."

"Then I say it was him who shot old Corkers, not any of your soldiers on the train."

But Tom allowed no clue to his own thoughts. He said, "We've another trespasser in the middle thicket."

"I didn't get a good look at him, neither, but I'll come back tomorrow and divine what I can."

When Tom gave him a worried look, Berkeley insisted, "You can't come back yourself, Mr Halls. Everyone knows as you hated old Corkers, so you can't be seen hereabouts for weeks and weeks."

"Berkeley, I can't trust you to keep quiet."

"You can, Mr Halls. You can."

"The more you do, the more you'll talk and you'll give our game away."

"You can trust me, Mr Halls." Then he added, "Sides, you've got no choice."

"I could finish you," Tom threatened. "Remember that, Boy. I could finish you off for good."

The boy grabbed the sleeve of Tom's poacher's jacket. "A motorcycle. Can you hear it, coming across the moor?"

"That's no bike," Tom snarled. He remembered, from years ago, the aspirated rattles of the Falcon engines as the 'Brisfits' had dusted woods where he lay hidden behind enemy lines. "It's a bloody aviator."

"It'll be one of the gentry from the flying club, come looking for old man Corkers."

"No. It's too weighty for sportsflying. No, it'll be the military."

"He's following the railway line. Mr Halls, has the alarm been shouted?"

But Tom was shaking his head. "He'll see nothing in the blackness, so what's he up to? Buggeration, what mess are we in the middle of?"

"There's horses on the trackbed, Mr Halls. I can hear them."

The two men stayed still, their eyes locked as they strained their ears.

"There!"

"There's nothing. Boy, you're thinking things up."

"But there is, Mr Halls, two of them. I can hear their sounds. Mr Halls, I do this every night, don't I? It's not Steward Orton. He'll come up from Home Farm and take the body away. He always does with his horse and cart, but it's not him yet." By now, he was weeping, his tears soaking his already smudged cheeks. He dragged a sleeve across his dribbling nose. "What will happen to us, Mr Halls?"

"Nothing, if we clear out. Keep to the woods, do you hear me?" Then Tom remembered the lad's blundering progress along the ridge. "When you get to the village, you don't go on either of the roads. You run silent, best you can, do you hear me, Boy Berkeley? And if you need to look round corners, you keep low, for God's sake. Now, can you get to your bed without waking your mother or father?"

"I do every night, don't I?" Then he asked, with the conscience of a fellow fugitive, "What'll you do, Mr Halls? You must hide, because they'll look for you straightaway."

Jessica Shipley, the strange woman of Larksteer Cottage, was up late because of the Pendlebury figures. She had promised that the

11

silhouettes would be ready before the 27th. Already, it was the 25th and Jessica saw little hope of cramming four days work into the next forty-eight hours. She had been at it since lunchtime; she was tired and had decided to clear the inks, brushes and empty milk stout bottles from the table. She straightened up, and an unladylike belch came up from her chest rather than the delicate innards of her little tummy. She felt dizzy. She looked at the other bottles on the hearth and decided to come back for them later, when she would feel better about bending down.

She liked to sleep in her kitchen. Every night she unrolled the mattress from the bottom of the larder and brought in two blankets that, during the day, were strewn across the great ramshackle couch in the front room. The mattress fitted exactly; the head nudged up against the stove door and the foot reached to the crockery cupboard. There was room to leave the stove door open on cold nights and the food in the larder was always temptingly naughty. Most nights, she had midnight feasts, sitting cross-legged on the mattress, or she would be greedy with fresh lemonade on the back doorstep. Sometimes she ate the whole night through, only to be sick in the morning. (She could neither understand it nor stop it but she prayed to be forgiven each Sunday.) Jessica Shipley slept downstairs because she was frightened of going up. She knew that her fears were punishment for being bad, so she kept quiet about them. If she told anyone, they'd only ask, "Then why have you chosen to live on your own in Larksteer Cottage, which has no road and can't be seen from anywhere else?" Jessica had tried to construct many different answers to this question. How could she explain that she wasn't frightened of the night or people – or even ghosts and bats? She kept a lantern burning on the weathered corner of her cottage, so that it could act as a beacon for folk lost on the moor in the dark. Strangers didn't worry her, but the thought of going upstairs to bed made her sick. So, why did she live here? The truth was plainly simple – no-one had invited her to live elsewhere.

Tom Hall was filthy. Keeping away from roads and houses, he reached Larksteer by crossing the wet moorland to the south of Thurrock's Farm. Black and freezing on a night like this. When he stopped to look across the valley, he saw lights on at the old Manor House and when he concentrated – his eyes getting used to distinguishing the shapes and shadows in the dark – he could even make out the figures assembling on the squire's courtyard. The alarm had been raised. Two miles west, he counted three sets of motor lamps progressing down Thurrock's track. One would be Dr Hawes' old Trèfle. Thank God, that the Boy Berkeley hadn't fled that way. Tom was exhausted; he was seven years older than the secret soldier of the Great War and a good deal less fit.

He was caught by surprise. The flyer came over the trees, three miles behind him, and coursed over the scrubland like a predator bird after its prey. A fluke of acoustics meant that Tom didn't hear the engine until the rush of wings was on his shoulders. He cursed and twisted, then covered his bare face and hands with his jacket. It wasn't as low as Tom feared, it never is, but the seven seconds, that he counted in his head to keep sane, left his heart racing. The pilot couldn't hope to spot a running man in this darkness, so what was going on?

His leggings were soaked. Dirt from the heath stuck to his face and hair. He'd lost a glove and grazed his knuckles until they bled. He knew that he'd cut his forehead and neck – and the old dig to his hip was playing up so badly that he completed the trek with the support of an iron rod that he'd found in one of the ruts.

"Old Corker's shot dead," he said before Jesse had properly opened the kitchen door.

At first, she seemed to make nothing of the news. She said, "Get your clothes off out there," as she folded the mattress away from the entrance. "You've got enough dirt on your flesh to plague my home for a month without you bringing more in on your clothes." As in all cases of Tom's disasters, she was sure that the least she knew, the better.

Forty minutes later, Tom was bathing in the front room. Jesse had got the log fire blazing and brought in pitchers of water, heated on the stove. "The Corker pulled up at Holt's Crossing, wanting me to break cover. We'd been playing cat and mouse for an hour, already. And in the end, there was me and him and three others. A man hiding in the lineside shed – he kept out of the Major's sight. Another man, running through the middle thicket, and the Boy Berkeley ..."

"Tom, I don't want to hear it. If I know too much, I'll let something slip and you'll be for it. I'm not a soldier, Tom. I'm a woman with a loose tongue in her head."

"This time, Jesse. This time, I need you to hear me out. I'm in deep trouble, girl, and you're the only one I trust. You've got to help me."

"It can't be like that and you know it; I'm a policeman's daughter."

"I don't care. God Jesse, they're going to think that I killed the old bastard."

"You've brought this on yourself, Tom Hall," she said, walking off to the scullery. "You've been saying that Eustace Corquet deserves to die for years. No-one believes that he shot your friend in the back. People know you'd never met the lad and Corquet wasn't even there."

"I never said."

"Yes, you did," she called through. "And much more and much too often." She came back and dropped a cake of coarse soap into his lap. "You need to go to her ladyship; she'll know what to do."

"Are you crazy?"

"I am not. Her ladyship won't see an innocent man in trouble and doesn't she know – more than anyone – that her husband was a wicked man?"

"She adores Mussolini," he snorted.

"Oh, I don't think she does!"

"She searches the newspapers for anything he's said or done."

"No, she doesn't," Jessica mocked. "And if she did, who says she's wrong? Mussolini wouldn't have coal strikes."

"Don't think she's holier than the rest of us, I'm saying, and don't call her 'ladyship' when she's not."

"She is round here. She has been ever since I was in Miss Carstairs' classroom. There's good charity in that lady, as well I know. Tom Hall, you'd know it too if you kept any thought of me in your heart."

The water was filthy in the tub and the soap seemed to be smearing grey dirt across his body rather than washing it off. Jessie replenished four earthenware jugs, then told him to stand up so that she could pour clean water over him. She thrust a floor-cloth into his hand and ordered that he should shield himself. The fresh water drenched him and he shook his head like a contented sire. "I'll cut the muck from your hair," she said, "and you can shave at the kitchen sink. You'll borrow some of father's old clothes from the staircase cupboard. Your own, I'll mend what I can but most of it's good for nothing but a bonfire."

"What have you seen tonight, Jesse?" he asked as he took a towel from her. "Who's been on the moor?"

"What do you mean 'tonight'? When was the Major hit?"

"Twenty minutes past midnight. No later."

"Then I don't want to answer any questions." She turned away; he was drying himself in a rough man's way that was too much even for a woman who had spent nights in the open with him. "I've been at my paintings since dinner-time and nothing else is my business."

But Tom persisted. "I saw the vicar. He'd been round here again, hadn't he? Sweet talking you, no doubt."

"Tom Hall, you know nothing about it."

"When did he leave, Jesse?"

"I don't know what you mean?" Still, she wasn't facing him.

"I was coming to see you. Then I spied the Reverend coming out of your yard and heading across the moor. I chased him. I wanted to catch him up and ask what he's about, always being here. But there was too much ground between us."

"Leave it be, Tom. You know nothing about it and look what your nosiness has already done tonight."

Tom came close to her, holding the towel to the front so that he wouldn't wet her. "When did the vicar leave you, Jesse?"

"Two hours before you said the Major was killed," she said, keeping her head to one side so that he couldn't kiss her.

"There's something going on in this house, Jesse. It's something upstairs, isn't it?"

"No, Tom. Honest."

"Don't tell me that. You've not been upstairs for a month. Jesse, when you tell me nothing's wrong, I don't believe you."

She brought her hands to her face. "I can't do it, Tom. I can't go up there." Then she pulled herself away and told him to dry his hair and shoulders, while she fetched her father's old clothes.

"Put them on," she said, before he could recover the conversation. "Then make for Lady Anne's and tell her all that's happened."

"The bugger, I will."

"You will," Jessie insisted. "And you'll ask her to hide you until things have quietened down. We'll not forget tonight, Tom Hall. Your foolishness has brought us to our crossroads. We can't go forward and, sure as the devil knows, we can't go back. You'll tell me there's other ways, but they look no more promising. 'Jessie and Tom', we're like two figures in a child's rhyme. Destined to carry on, just as we are. Up the hill to fetch our pails of water. Not one thing and not the other. Except, from tonight, we can't wish our own futures, can we?"

Twenty minutes later, Jessie stood at the corner of her back yard and watched the poor figure walk unsteadily into the night. He crossed the ditch of brambles and her last sight of him had him stumbling over the hardcore of some old workings. His hip was hurting badly, she knew. Dawn was less than an hour away, hardly enough time for him to make the old Manor House in the dark.

CHAPTER TWO

At one in the afternoon, when the sun was shining through the loft window, the parish policeman stayed in bed and watched the farmer's bare wife collect her clothes from a chair in the corner. Properly, he should have closed his eyes but Constable Pinch was in a hard-done-by mood, so he damned the world and took a look. Edna Thurrock, from behind, was out of shape, as pale as musty pearl and blotched with red and brown places. Pinch decided that the limbs on her left side were longer than the others so that her back and shoulders had to lean to put things right. Her hips rocked like a coracle on choppy waters and her podgy bottom moved like two lumps of porridge in a boiling pan. Her ankles and elbows had been rubbed red – she was a woman who worked too long in harsh water. And her back and the backs of her legs bore a scatter shot of brown moles. Some were hairy and others were broken. The biggest one was a rusty colour and grew exactly on the spot that, Pinch calculated, would be squashed by all her weight when she sat down. Perhaps that was why it was flat and had spread to twice the size of the others.

Nevertheless, Farmer Thurrock's wife's bottom was a lovely one and Pinch wanted his last look at it to be a good one, so he tucked his chin further beneath the comfortably worn linen where the fluff tickled his nose and his idle policeman's eyes could peep over the stitched hem of the blankets. She's succulent, he wanted to say; succulent, well-bottomed and blessed with an earthiness that stayed with Pinch for hours after he had bedded her.

She dressed out of sight, on the landing. "Don't be long," she warned. "Thurrock will be in, any moment." Then he heard the clunk-clunk of her footsteps going downstairs. Edna Thurrock wasn't a dainty woman.

He was supposed to follow her promptly so that they both could be dressed and ready when her husband appeared in the kitchen, but Pinch was in an awkward mood, so he took his time.

"Cross," he grumbled to himself.

He knew that people would be looking for him. The Chief Constable had already assured Reverend Beamish that the parishioners would see their policeman out and about during this anxious time. He should be standing at the church gate at the top of the village, or half-way down the hill by the War Memorial or at the schoolyard where the street crossed the narrow river. But Pinch called it all poppycock. Murder had been done on his beat, yet he had not been told until seven in the morning when the sentries were already in place and Pinch had not been allowed to pass. What nonsense! 'Keep your ear to the ground, our Pinch' the Chief Constable had said. 'Report all the gossip.' Well, never mind the Chief Constable. Pinch knew that he was worth more than that and he would waste no time listening to the notions and accusations of the village toffs and their witch-wives. He'd rather enjoy a comfy bed in Edna Thurrock's loft. Pinch had promised to meet his daughter at Larksteer Cottage that afternoon, but he would be late for that too; he was determined to be late. Other people thought that he should be out looking for Tom Hall. Well, hey-ho to that as well.

"Cross," he repeated. "But don't know what to do about it."

And that was Pinch's problem. So often, when he got cross, he made a mess of things.

Already, the fowls were scuttling away as Thurrock carried his bucket and shovel across the yard. The house dog would be sitting up straight, wanting her master to fondle her head as he scraped the mud from his boots.

Pinch sat on the edge of the bed, wiped his private parts with a corner of the coarse blanket, and grunted as he picked up his clothes from the floor.

He hesitated at the top of the stairs. His rough swarthy face was still tacky with bed-sweat, his breathing was heavy with old tobacco and his fingers felt fat and sausage-like. He looked down, like a drunk who's uncertain of making the journey. He promised himself that he would speak as soon as he opened the scullery door, getting in before the husband had chance to complain. So, Pinch had thirteen steps down to conjure up a knock-out phrase.

Harold Thurrock, standing at the window and not looking at his wife who had found something to do in a far corner, heard the middle stair creak. His hand reached for two wooden tankards on the windowsill and he filled them with warm ale from the barrel beside the sink. The blood on the back of his hand had dried hard and deep red, a thread that sat proud of his skin. It looked false. It looked like a heavy cosmetic scar glued to an actor in a melodrama.

When he heard Pinch at the other side of the door, Thurrock turned to face the room with a beer in each hand and, as Pinch entered, the farmer proposed, "My thanks to you, Pinch!" and raised a beaker.

Edna was crouching on her hands and knees and seemed to make herself even more busy so that she could keep her back to the men. Pinch looked, enough to take away another picture of her mature rear end but not, he thought, enough to get caught.

"I want ... we both want to thank you," Harold Thurrock was saying. "Edna has told you there's no need for you to visit again?"

Pinch nodded. He promised to keep clear in the coming months. "I'll make nothing of the baby when it comes. It will be Farmer Thurrock's issue. That was what we said."

By now, Pinch had only to draw breath and his vulgar voice filled Edna's head. It sucked, rumbled and spat like rotting rats cooking on hot coals and, when she knew that she couldn't close her ears to it, she wanted to scream.

"You're a good man, Pinch," said Thurrock and Edna's throat went tight. She closed her eyes and drew in deep as she heard her husband say, "We ... it has been difficult for you, difficult for us all, but Edna and I know you're an honest and good man."

Weeks before, when husband and wife had discussed the proposal at this kitchen table, with Pinch listening in, Harry had promised that they could hardly be the first couple to solve their problem in this way. It must go on every thirty years or so, Harry had said. "And in every village in England, I'd say." Only now, for all of Harry's brave face, Edna and Harry weren't sure that bringing in Pinch had been for the best; the price had been unforgivably high.

"You've injured your hand?" Pinch asked.

"It got bit by a casting on a shed door." Thurrock seemed to swallow some more words before he continued. "I've been down to the lineside this morning. There's plenty of soldiers there; they didn't like me being about but I wanted to see things for myself. Corkers was a neighbour – like him or damn him – and it doesn't do for a man to have his neighbour slain without knowing the ins and outs of it. The door to the engineers' hut caught me unaware as I was closing it up." He looked at the scar on his hand.

Edna Thurruck had stomached more than she could take. She buried her face in her hands and, without straightening her back, ran from the house.

"People will ask questions," Pinch warned, while the noise of the woman's going was still fresh in the air.

"Why ever should they? Folk round here know that Edna and I have been wanting a family. What could be more expected than her happy condition?"

"I don't mean babies. I mean murder. People will want to know where you were last night."

There was only a moment's hesitation, no more than a flicker of anxiety across Thurrock's creased and yellow face, but it was enough to convince Pinch that Farmer Thurrock had been twice the fool: he had been close when the murder was done and, this morning, he had returned to clean up.

The tracks from Thurrock's Farm to St Stephen's church, where Pinch had tethered his bicycle, were uphill and wet and, for five hundred yards, Pinch made little progress as he skirted the fields and avoided a soddened corner more suitable for water buffalo than downland sheep. He passed through three gates, crossed more makeshift bridges and gradually established a good distance between him and Harry and Edna's home. He kept an eye out to his right; a solitary sentry and an ancient army ambulance were the only presence at Holt's Crossing but Pinch had no mind to go there. He was sure that he could learn more by surveying the broad layout of the land than a detailed examination of the murder scene. (He'd leave that to the experts; they'd get nowhere.) Of course, Pinch knew the ground well but he wanted to stop and stare – he needed to picture what could have gone on – and he couldn't do that, properly, until he was half-way up the hill.

After twenty minutes, Pinch seemed hardly to have started his climb. His boots were heavy with mud, his ears were red and he knew that worse was to come. If Pinch didn't want to walk down the village street, looking like a remnant from a football match, he needed to take preventative measures. He leant against a disabled gatepost, looked around – not once, but two or three times – then set about taking off his boots and socks. And his helmet. And he unbuttoned his tunic. And then he rolled his trouser legs up to his knees. He put the socks in the boots and tied the laces to the strap of his helmet so that the bundle could be swung from one hand.

He pressed on.

He wanted to reach a point where, with good height and distance, he could capture Thurrock's likely route from the farm to Holt's Crossing. Pinch already knew that two men (or three?) had been hiding in the woods along Holt's Ridge when old Corquet was done in. What view would they have had of Thurrock's expedition? And what about the trundling train? What difference would that have made?

But things weren't working out for Pinch. The rolled up trouser legs kept slipping down and he would be muddied to the eyes before long. He thought about taking his trousers off – but that would have been too ridiculous! He decided to make for the Idling Pool, sixty yards from the trees of Holt's Ridge, and take stock from there. So, he left the track and crossed the treacherous furrows of turned soil. He stumbled and lurched. He hung his boots and helmet around his neck. Twice, his hands reached out to stop him falling full length in the dirt.

21

He found that the Idling Pool was full and leafy. It had made marshy ground on its lee side but, just a dozen yards away, where a rock wanted to break through the earth, Pinch found a saucer of dry ground. Mercy! He sat down, laid his socks out to dry, and started to clean his boots with handfuls of long grass. He was comfortable now but, he started to be bothered by a curious memory. That notion of taking off his trousers had started it and, although he pushed the thoughts to the back of his mind, he couldn't be free of them. Sometime or other, he had enjoyed the sensation of rubbing his cold seat in long grass. He couldn't remember where or when and he couldn't swear that it was properly remembered; yet, he couldn't get rid of the feeling.

Well! He couldn't go that far, but he could reasonably take off his uniform trousers, soak any mud from the legs and stretch them out on the ground. Indeed, he argued, he had little choice; he could hardly patrol the village in his present state.

Pinch dressed down to his shirt.

"The King's Peace," he recited boldly, "is an honourable state, drawn from man's will for civilised behaviour. It is the natural order of society and any interruption of that is a breach of the peace."

He sat down. The long grass was lovely. It was fresh and moist. It tickled and chilled. If Pinch closed his eyes, he could pretend that he was a child again. What was it? What was this memory that begged him so strongly?

Pinch's daily routine allowed little opportunity for fun. He rarely shared his sense of humour because he couldn't see how a chap could without making himself vulnerable. Laughing may not be a weakness but provoking it must surely be. Only when Punch was alone – and sure that he could not be watched – did he play the clown. Then, sometimes, he would make an idiot of himself in his own clumsy, untalented, unfunny way.

"Outrageous murder!" he shouted. "Done on the railway line with -" he stretched out his hands "- my Jessica's cottage and Thurrock's Farm far off to my right, while Holt's Ridge, to my left, bears down upon the scene. The audience mounted o'er the colosseum. Men's will," he repeated. "Mens Rea, the doctrine of the guilty mind." Then he joked, "Men's Rear!" and joggled his rump on the ground. "Guilty pleasures in mind. And running home, where did they go? Thurrock the Farmer withdrew, out of sight. Tom Hall – playing Tom, Tom the Fool – runs across the moor to my Jessica's refuge. But anyone else," he clambered to his feet and pushed both hands forward, like a surveyor designing his highway, "this way, with me, to the village."

But his playful monologue was scuppered when he spotted a lady's cigarette lighter carefully placed on a tree stump, ten yards away. "Put your trousers and socks on, Pinch," he said.

He noted that it could not have fallen like this. It must have been lost, then found by a passer-by and put on show for its owner to find. Pinch, half-dressed and beginning to feel the cold, turned it over in his hand. He flicked it alight, then snapped it shut. Then, knowing where it had come from, he polished its shiny surface on the seat of his trousers.

He was in the middle of doing this, when he saw something move in the trees. He took a step forward, bent at his waist, and stuck his neck out. "Was that a glitter of sunshine on polished metal?" he asked himself. "My word, Pinch, have we been spotted?" The spy ran off through the woods and Pinch was in no state to chase him. He rubbed his chin. "Sooner or later, my boy, we'll hear a story of Pinch playing in the long wet grass."

Peggy Pinch liked to do her verges between three o'clock and half past because that's when the most interesting people walked by. At the top of the hill, Clemency Carstairs was practising with the church doors open and *Nearer My God to Thee* was tumbling down the village. The young Mrs Willowby, across the road and twenty yards up from the Police House, tried to keep pace with the melody but she wasn't up to it. "Can't you sing along?" she called through an open window, "Help me, Peggy." But Peggy wouldn't respond. She didn't approve of the new fad, shouting from houses and across the road. It wasn't a question of good or bad manners; it was a matter of keeping quiet. Villages had been quiet for hundreds of years, Peggy believed, so that should be taken as the right way to be. Besides, tittle-tattle became vicious and rude at too high a volume. All good gossip should be delivered quietly, eye to eye – and the prospect of good gossip was why she was here. In a few minutes, the town bus – with its solid rubber tyres, removable winter windows and twenty-five seats arranged in five rows to include the driver – would bring back the shoppers from the weekly market. The vehicle would rattle and choke as it climbed the country lane, hardly achieving half of the twelve miles per hour limit. 'Shall we walk home?' went the village joke. 'Why? We're in no hurry so let's take the bus.' There was one trip in the morning, returning at teatime (but not Tuesdays and Fridays).

That afternoon, Peggy was counting on Jasmine Moorcroft's sister, Muriel, to bring the latest news from the Tea Rooms, so she was on her knees at the front flowerbed when Inspector York parked his motorcycle in the narrow pull-in beyond the front gate. She had been working without her gloves, wanting her fingers to dig out the roots of the dock leaves, and some of the soil had got into her hair.

"Why, Inspector York. Good afternoon."

"A guess?" The inspector had not expected that he would be recognised in the village.

"Not really." Peggy pressed her hands to her aching back as she sat up straight. "You were in town last night, asking questions in the Crown. My husband heard all about you from Miss Hestey before he'd finished his breakfast. Miss Hestey comes round while Pinch sits over his three poached eggs each morning. Sometimes, Pinch says that he learns more at his breakfast table than he does for the rest of the day."

Peggy considered the inspector's appearance. Carlton York was a small man who wore two cardigans under his jacket. He liked wool ties and knitted scarves. (Peggy counted four different colours in the five days before the murderer was caught.) She guessed that Mr York was a delicate child who had never grown out of it. At first, she was surprised that he preferred a motorcycle to a car, but York travelled alone and like to appear at places unexpected.

24

Motorbikes suited him. During the next week, Peggy learned to respect, fear and, in the end, despise this man. There was something secret about him. For all the marks of conservatism and establishment, people never knew what he was about. 'I don't know what he'll bring to our village,' Miss Hestey had remarked at breakfast. 'But I'm sure we don't need it.'

"Miss Hestey described you very well," she said.

"I need to talk with your husband, Mrs Pinch."

"He won't be back until six o'clock. He's very busy this afternoon. He's walking the railway line where the murder was done. He may not be a detective, Inspector York, but he knows his duties well."

"Then I've two hours to wait."

"The Red Lion will look after you very well, I'm sure."

"And who will I meet there?" He teased, "Mr Meggastones the verger, Orton the steward of Home Farm, Ben Tucker who may be hired at any time?"

"He's best as a thatcher," Peggy said.

"What about Tom Hall? Will I meet him in the Red Lion?"

"Inspector, you know very well you won't."

"You went to school with Tom Hall?" he asked.

"I did. Across the road, you'll see the very classroom, next to Miss Carstairs' cottage. She was our teacher, and so well thought of that the panel gave her let of the school cottage on her retirement."

"So, you know Tom well?"

Peggy looked across the road as the rickety bus pulled up by the hedgerow. David the driver would be wanting a cup of tea from someone, she thought. Dolly Hoskins saw that Peggy was busy talking so she waved politely and went off to bother the postmistress. But Muriel Moorcroft wanted to know what was going on. She stood in the middle of The Street, nodding, wanting Peggy and her visitor to carry on talking. Miss Carstairs, striding home from the church, saw what nosy Muriel was up to and told her to follow her indoors. "We'll make tea for Driver David. He'll be wanting a cuppa."

When The Street had settled down, Peggy continued, "There

wasn't a man in the village who was better on stilts. That was before the war, of course. He got badly hurt in France."

"But you know more about him than that," York insisted.

"We all know Tom, as well as he knows all of us. You'll get nowhere asking questions about Tom Hall. Everyone in the village knows that he didn't kill Major Corquet, and asking questions won't help you find him. He was a scout in the Great War and he can survive in the countryside for weeks and not show himself. Let it be known that he's not suspected of murder and he'll come forward soon enough."

"Can you help me with that?"

"Pinch will," she said. "Very well."

"You don't think I ought to come in?"

"Ordinarily. If you were from County, I'd show you the registers, wouldn't I? Pinch doesn't expect me to wait for him. Not for things like that." (Indeed, Pinch knew that he was no good at housekeeping, so he relied on his wife to take on those affairs. Not that he had ever asked for her help.)

"I understand, your husband wouldn't like to find his wife serving tea and nattering to a senior detective. So far, but no further, perhaps?"

"A constable's wife needs to be careful. She could easily say things that upset."

"You can tell me when you last saw Thomas Hall, surely?"

"I'm sorry," she said, and for a moment York thought she was saying no. "I've been rude. Mr Pinch and I would love you to stay for tea. Dolly Hoskins has baked some fresh scones and she's given us far more than we Pinches could eat. She's a dear lady but," Peggy confided in a subdued voice, "let me tell you a secret about Dolly's cooking. Her fancies don't last. Please wait a moment." Peggy collected herself, entered the house through the scullery door and emerged at the front door to let the inspector in.

They walked through the tidy Police House and settled in the parlour. "Mr Pinch likes to sit with his back to the window, so if you comfy yourself in the other armchair, a dining chair from the hall will be very suitable for me."

That arranged, and knowing that Pinch wouldn't be a couple of hours but would be home in a few minutes, Peggy excused herself to the kitchen and the business of making tea. When she peeped, Inspector York was looking at the display of photographs on the polished sideboard. There were pictures of Pinch as a distinguished scholarship boy, with the vicar on last year's Memorial Day, on parade at County Headquarters, and hand in hand with his grown-up daughter, Jessica. Peggy was Pinch's bride in a small one at the back.

Peggy looked at her packet of cigarettes on the windowsill, and at her favourite spot (the back doorstep) and wondered if she would have enough time to smoke. Then she heard Pinch lean his bicycle against the back wall and stoop over a drain as he took off his trouser clips.

"Inspector York is here," she said quietly when his face appeared in the kitchen.

"I know that from his motorcycle out the front."

York had stayed on his feet. He introduced himself and offered his hand. At once, the constable identified that this detective was too short to ever have been a patrolling policeman, so he must have enlisted in CID directly from another profession. It was not a promising start to their collaboration.

"My uniform is not as sharp as it might be," Pinch announced to stall any criticism. "I've been trudging the ground. Of course, it would have been better if I had not been kept beyond bounds at the start."

"Yes, I need to explain that."

"A woman was in the middle thicket last night," said Pinch, determined to keep ahead of the detective. "Some time between seven-thirty and this morning's rain."

"A poacher?"

Peggy carried a tea tray into the parlour. "Polly Gunn is our petticoat poacher around here," she remarked, then immediately realised that she had spoken out of turn.

"Yes, well," frowned her husband. "I don't think we need question Miss Gunn about murder, do you?"

27

"Please, I need to explain," the inspector repeated.

"I – need to find things to do," Peggy whispered. "I shall be at my flowerbeds, if you need me."

But Peggy didn't go to the garden. She busied herself with crockery and cultery that she had brought to the house on her wedding day. She laid doillies on a trolley, as Miss Carstairs had taught her after one Sunday School, and she provided the tea with not too much and not too little sweets and savouries. She took her time.

"The Great Strike seems inevitable," she heard the inspector say. "Personally, I believe that both sides have their minds so set on confrontation that no amount of talking will change anything, until they – the owners and the grand amalgamation – have tested each other's strength. Some people say that a strike will be a good thing; it will sort matters out, once and for all. But wiser heads see danger in such widespread disobedience. There is a fear of insurrection."

"You mean a revolution?" asked her husband.

She pictured the inspector, raising a reassuring hand. "Nothing that the military isn't more than adequate to meet. Little pockets, perhaps, that will be put down before night falls. But a number of us – detectives with particular experiences – have been asked to keep watch. Your county falls within my region of affairs."

"I don't have a county, Inspector. Just a small village on a hillside and half a valley of farmland."

Peggy went to the airing cupboard, which shared a back wall with the old stove, and checked that her nightdress was warming thoroughly. She went to the larder and turned the butter and bread on the marble slab. All these things she could do – as every housewife learned – with enough noise to say that she was keeping busy, but without disturbing the talk in the parlour.

"Pinch, I have to wonder if Corquet's death could be a political matter," Mr York said.

Pinch leaned forward and said the words slowly, "You think he was assassinated? Good Lord above."

"We know that Corquet would have been one of the early targets for any revolutionaries, and one of your parishioners has been very vocal in his dissatisfaction."

Peggy, hiding behind the door, muttered to herself, "Tom Hall again."

"You mean Hall," Pinch confirmed. "He's not been seen since Farmer Thurrock brought in his cows, yesterday afternoon. I was asked to check on comings and goings; Tom Hall was the first name I attended to."

"Where would he hide?"

"Jessica Shipley is his best friend, I would say, at Larksteer Cottage but he wouldn't have gone to her. He'd know that we'd look there first."

Peggy hesitated at the door. When both men looked her way, she stepped forward. "The vicar has been very kind with his damsen jam. I'm sure we are first to have a pot. Here, I've put some on the trolley."

"Jessica Shipley is my daughter," said Pinch. "Stay with us, Peggy. Sit on the chair and share some scones."

The inspector was embarrassed. The constable's tone had suggested that he intended his wife to endure an uncomfortable conversation.

"My first wife committed suicide in 1914," Pinch continued, although no further question had been asked. "Jessica blames me, so she has taken her mother's natural name. The circumstances are well known in the village, and to the Chief Constable. Peggy, I think the inspector would like a napkin for his jam."

York coughed lightly. "Please, I didn't mean to pry."

"I'm sure," smiled Pinch. "We can also tell you that Major Corquet owed money. We can say that, can't we, Peggy? Peggy, tell the inspector all about it."

Peggy began hesitantly. This was something unrehearsed. "Last Thursday, I was forgotten in the church for almost twenty minutes. I had promised to clean the Georgian tiles with Miss Hestey but she went home early while I carried on working behind the wall tapestry. That's when the Major and Reverend Beamish came in."

"Be aware when my wife is in hiding, Inspector York. She eavesdrops."

"Oh, that's unfair. I couldn't help but overhear."

29

But Pinch's grin declared that he was right and she was wrong; he often grinned that way.

"What did they say, Mrs Pinch?" the inspector asked.

"Major Corquet was at his wit's end, sir. He said that he couldn't possibly pay the money and he hoped that the vicar would intervene."

" 'Couldn't possibly pay'," echoed the detective. "How could he have expected the vicar to help?"

PC Pinch explained. "He's a sort of unofficial bench, round here. Telling people how they can make amends for what they've done wrong. Simple misdemeanors, you understand."

"The vicar gives out punishments?" asked an incredulous Inspector York.

Peggy shook her head. "Good works, usually. Extra effort for the parish, that's how our Reverend sees it. That's what was behind his taking on of Polly Gunn; she's the morning maid at the vicarage now." She added, "We are a very secluded parish, Inspector, and our vicar is a good and devout man."

The inspector was rubbing his chin. " 'Couldn't possibly pay'," he repeated thoughtfully. "Was the Major in debt? I think he was being blackmailed."

Half past five was teatime in the parish and all its souls drew breath. The Street and Back Lane were empty, children had been called in and the shops, though open, were unattended. Neither Thurrock nor Jones drove cattle through the village at this time. The church attendants carried on working, for evensong was only forty minutes away, and sometimes Pinch would stand at the War Memorial, but these activities seemed to support the community's restfulness rather than disrupt it. There was something satisfying about the quiet, as if everyone's labour had produced a peace that, naturally, belonged to them all. Mrs Dorrick, who rarely ate after two in the afternoon, sat back and reviewed her day's knitting, stretching a growing sleeve, smoothing out some ribbing or merely feeling the satisfying textures of knitted landscape without a dropped stitch. Professor Malling, an entomologist of private means, returned to the crossword that he had started over breakfast, while Mrs Willowby washed three grubby faces and wet and combed their hair in readiness for Mr Willowby's return from an office in the nearby market town.

The sun was sinking behind the churchyard elms and the coolness brought out the true scents of the wayside. Pinch in uniform stood at ease in front of the stone plinth, acknowledging the bonneted and booted (none less than fifty years old) by lifting himself onto the balls of his feet. The men who walked past the memorial lifted their hats. Peggy and Pinch went to church twice on Sundays and once during the week, usually a Wednesday evensong. These were the only times that they were seen together in the village. Peggy, who had lived all her life in The Street, had interests that couldn't include her husband. Most of the gatherings were, he thought, small-minded women's affairs but he suspected that many of her morning rounds and afternoon teas discussed intimacies that a man wouldn't understand. 'Women's Business' had always been a mystery to him, problems and ailments that, his grandfather had advised, were better left untouched.

That evening, Pinch stayed at the War Memorial until eight o'clock. He wanted to satisfy himself that York was doing no snooping. Also, he was conscious that any superior officers visiting the murder scene but staying overnight in the next town, would probably pass through the village. The parish constable could do himself no harm, being seen out and about. He watched a flock of sheep, driven down the lane by Ben Tucker on a bicycle with a whippy stick that looked nothing like a shepherd's crook. Pinch followed, saluting the vicar who was on his way up on the other side.

Before bedtime, sitting in his favourite armchair, Pinch looked up from his newspaper and asked, "What did you tell him?"

"I said you wanted to walk along the railway line where the Major died," said Peggy. "I thought, it's the sort of work that could take two minutes or two hours, so you could easily explain being away from the village."

"Yes, that's clever."

"Pinch, I meant you could say what you've been up to and make it as long or as short as you like."

"Yes, yes. I understand."

"Do you ..."

"Yes?"

"Well, I do think it's wrong to say that the Major was being blackmailed. It sounded to me that he was offering money. The vicar wasn't demanding it. In fact, he spoke as if he wanted to say no to it. I was thinking, you could put the inspector straight."

Pinch raised the newspaper so that it obscured his face. "I think we'll leave those matters to the inspector. After all, no-one wants to involve PC Pinch. Not least, PC Pinch himself."

"Oh, Pinch. Do try. He seems much more important than the superior officers from round here."

"An important person, you say. Yet you spoke to him of our petticoat poacher."

"I know. I'm sorry. I didn't think. I didn't mean ..."

"Commonly so," said the husband. "By the way, our arrangement with the Thurrocks."

"Yes?"

"They won't need our help from now on."

"You mean, she's having your baby?"

"Their baby, Peggy. It was always going to be their baby. She told me the good news before I left, this afternoon."

Suddenly, he laid the paper aside. "Peggy, you will not look at me with reproach. Didn't I pray for guidance? For three months, I didn't agree to help this unfortunate couple until I was sure it was the right course to take. At home with nature's good law. Honourable and decent."

Peggy and Pinch did not usually show their bodies to each other. Pinch went up first while Peggy undressed in the kitchen because her nightdress was always airing there. She took her time. Sometimes, she felt that she would pay money to stay downstairs (but then, she joked to herself, Pinch would want to know where she had got it from). She always made sure that Pinch was in pyjamas, with the

32

light off, before she walked into the bedroom. Sometimes, she liked to read in bed but she never switched on the lamp until she was safely in. Perhaps their married life did not have to be like this, but Pinch had never asked for it to be any different.

She didn't want to sleep with him that night, but Pinch was too much like Pinch to sense it. "Miss Carstairs is calling for that cat again," she said, collecting her detective novel as she climbed between the sheets. "She's silly to worry this early." Then, brightly: "You must be very pleased with the way that the village has coped." But they both knew that there would be no conversation.

Pinch turned his back and belched three times in ten minutes. (He always did, so how could Peggy complain tonight?) Then he grumbled about her bedside lamp so that she had to stop reading before she had finished her chapter. He didn't speak again. Peggy knew that his daughter liked to call him the Grunting Pig, recalling the noises he had made when he napped on the parlour couch during her childhood; but Peggy had learned that things were worse than that. He made noises only when he was half asleep. Peggy knew that he had properly gone off when one big toe began to itch the sock from the other foot. Then the second big toe would do it to the first foot. Then Pinch stretched his legs and sometimes arched his back like a beast with indigestion, leaving Peggy with only a cold margin of the mattress. He'd scratch himself. He'd pinch and tug at his ear, and wipe his face. He was too lazy to get out in the night. If he needed to go, he would stubbornly refuse to wake up and, in his sleep, he would hold himself or try to curl up like a baby or, taking all the bed, lie on his back and tense his tummy and thigh muscles. He knew nothing about this. He talked in his sleep only when he had been patrolling alone late at night and had started conversations in his head that needed finishing off. (This was how Peggy learned, before anyone else in the village, that Mrs Gunn had been summoned by her sick father to Bolton, and Miss Hestey had drunk herself silly at her back fence. For several weeks, Pinch had spoken of a Black Prince, but Peggy couldn't work out who he was. It couldn't be a pub because Pinch said he would move with grace and candour.) Of course, Pinch broke wind without knowing it, not mightily so but in little phuts that went on and on, as if he were having a conversation with himself at the wrong end. Then there were nights when, lying on his side, Pinch would lift one leg as if he needed to let some air in. He didn't do this every night, but if he did, the top leg would go up and down all night. But, worst of all, was the scratching. Peggy couldn't stand it.

At half past one in the morning, she left the bedroom.

She took her housecoat from a hook on the kitchen door, collected her cigarettes from the cutlery drawer and sat on the back step.

Cigarettes had been there in so many of her peaceful moments. Smoking wasn't her secret habit but neither was she one of the bright young things who puffed away in public and held their cigarettes like exhibits. Those ladies in advertisements seemed to express themselves with particular brands, almost showing off, but Peg was content for tobacco to bring on her solitude. Night-time outside was a favourite time of day. No chores were waiting, there were no chattering neighbours, and she knew where Pinch was and what he was up to. This was a moment to count her blessings. She wouldn't let the cold and drizzle spoil the peace of smoking a cigarette like this. Neither, the occasional breeze that fluttered down the side path and made a nuisance with her coat and nightie. The village street was just a dozen yards away but she expected no traffic. Unusually, she might see the dark figure of someone walking home but they wouldn't call out. And sometimes she would hear Tubby Stoker stacking bottles and crates in the back yard of The Red Lion or, if the night was especially quiet and the wind was right, she might hear the opening and closing of St Stephen's great door as someone went in to pray.

Then she noticed the bowl of vegetable peelings at the bottom of the garden. Pinch had promised to mix them with the compost but other matters had distracted him. And there they were, left on the side of the path. As she stared at the waste, a naughty idea germinated in her mind.

Inside the house and three steps down from the kitchen was a stone passage not eight feet long. The heavy door on the right, with its strong brass handle, and a top and bottom bolt, shut off the cold cell, where drunks and vagabonds could be locked in overnight when it was too late to take them to the town's police station. The little cell block had been built with heavy thick walls, no windows and a double door so that the noise of a violent drunk would not trouble the rest of the house. But Peggy had never known her husband use this part of the Police House for its proper purpose. Sometimes, he stored pungent hooch in the cells. Once, she had tried to adopt the space to launder linen but this had made Pinch so angry that she never tried to take such obvious possession of it again.

On the threshold of the passage, floorcloths, dishcloths, mopheads and a lavatory brush had been soaking in soda since breakfast time. Peggy carried the heavy tub to the yard where she laid the cloths and brushes on the stone slabs. Then she mixed the potato peelings with the dirty water and stirred in a jug of curdled milk.

CHAPTER THREE

It would be several weeks before Edna Thurrock's good news could be traded across the garden gates and public footpaths of the village. Jasmine Moorcroft, whose mature and bulbous nose was known to have the best sense of a woman's condition, didn't give the farmer's wife a second look as, on the morning of Peggy Pinch's naughty idea, she crossed the rutted brick and sod track of Back Lane. October Cottage was being re-thatched and the narrow way was obstructed with horsecarts and handbarrows. Jasmine was sure that crafty Ben Tucker was spending too long looking over people's hedges and attending less to his pegging. "Heaven knows where his lad is," she complained as she bowled past Edna.

If the village street was ever busy, it was in the morning. The women wore three-quarter length dresses and dowdy overcoats, and everyone wore a hat. If two, or sometimes three, chose to talk to one another, they stood in the middle of the carriageway rather than at the dirty edges, for there was little chance of traffic. (It would have seemed rather vulgar for four women to meet in that way; like an unnecessary crowd.) Normally, manners and form had much to do with village life; it wouldn't do to unsettle things, but the murder had put people on edge.

Talk in the Post Office set the Thurrock pulse racing.

"Certain people are spending too long with certain other people," observed Mistress Hestey.

"Like all day Monday, I've heard," agreed the postmistress. "Oh my! Mrs Thurrock, we didn't see you there. How may I help?"

Miss Hestey persisted, "Well, somebody might think it proper to inform a certain high office."

Edna asked nervously for a small packet of mantles. She thought, they can't have heard about Pinch's afternoons at the farm.

Clemency Carstairs, the old schoolma'am who had entered the shop in time to hear Miss Hestey's remarks, put her wicker shopping basket on the counter. "If," she said. "If you are thinking of complaining to the bishop about our good vicar's behaviour, you'd be well advised that there is a local circle that properly receives such enquiries. Not," she said, unwrapping string from a paper bag, "not the poison pen of an old gossip. This string is faulty."

"Oh, you're a wicked woman, Clemency Carstairs, to call me a poison pen. When all I said ..."

"All you meant, was that Reverend Beamish spends too long at Larksteer Cottage."

"I never said! I said 'certain persons'. Edna Thurrock, didn't I say 'certain persons'?"

Edna picked up her gas mantles and her change and said that she couldn't recall exactly what was said, before retracting herself from the muddle. She stepped into The Street, sticky and flustered, and she told herself off. When her good news is properly announced, no-one will suspect that Thurrock wasn't the real father, but being bothered by gossip in a Post Office queue is just the sort of silly behaviour that would be remarked upon.

Ben Tucker, with straw coming out of his shirt, walked past her, briefly taking off his cap as he crossed in front of the War Memorial. Edna was conscious of his saying, "Good morning, Mrs Pinch," but before Edna could turn around, her hat had been whipped away and a flush of goo spilled down on her head.

She yelled, and then came a second dollop, cold and smelly and dribbling to all her places. She was on her knees before she knew it, fingering the mess to work out what it was. "My hair, it's soaked in it," she cried, bewildered and desperate. "My eyes and down my front. I – I can't see!"

Then the Pinch woman's hands were on her shoulders and the younger woman's face came close to hers.

"Deceitful strumpet!" Peg spat in a low voice.

Edna's fingers were so pasty that she dared not touch her clothes or wipe her face. "Deceitful? I don't ..."

The Pinch-wife whispered into the woman's clogged up ear. "You took my husband to your bed when you knew that you were already carrying. So what was it? A big thank you? Something to remember you by? Or was it just once more for luck? You filthy, filthy woman."

"Oh God, but this? Have you had the smell of it?" She was putting each fingertip beneath her nostrils. "It's sour. It's suds of ... God, it's foul." She was heavy with it. Still, she couldn't see properly. She hadn't thought to put her bodice straight and everything felt soiled. She could tell that a heel had broken from one shoe.

Miss Carstairs and Miss Hestey, Ben Tucker and old man St John were running towards them. "Get Pinch! Pinch must be told!" Miss Hestey shouted, over and over. The postmistress had locked up and ran to catch them up.

The others looked after the farmer's wife but Miss Carstairs put her arm around Peggy's shoulder and led her away. "Pinch will hear soon enough," she said. Already she was walking Peggy up the hill. "Don't upset yourself."

Peggy felt all the faces at the cottage windows, and the stares from the road's edge. It was as if her misdemeanor had put the village into a tilt, spilling everyone from back rooms to front rooms, from garden sheds to garden gates, from shop counters to shop doorways.

"Upset?" chuckled Peggy, short of breath. "I'm thrilled, Miss Carstairs."

The schoolma'am allowed a little heaviness to creep into her voice. "Well, let's get you out of the way because a great many people might think that you shouldn't be."

"Thrilled," she repeated.

"You forget that I have known Peggy Pinch since she was four years old. I stood over her when she chalked her computations on her school slate. I listened to her first recitations. And I watched her pretty dance steps. This morning's show tells me that Peggy Pinch is at the end of her tether. They're having an affair, I take it."

"Not an affair. Not in the way you mean."

"Then we have a good start, at least. Has he taken his belt to you?"

"No! Pinch has never laid a hand on me. I do wish people would stop thinking it." But she added, "You know that he gets very drunk."

"Yes. I think we all know that. There are nights when the Red Lion will only give him beer in their garden and, one morning last Winter, I found him drunk and asleep in the churchyard. But, even when he's drunk, he won't hit you?"

Peggy shook her head. She was aware that she was on the edge of weeping, and told herself off for it. "Really, I'm fine."

"But he can be very insistent on those occasions?" asked Miss Carstairs.

"No," Peggy said frankly. "He's never insistent."

She looked to her old teacher for a cue. Miss Carstairs nodded, so slightly that the movement could hardly be noticed.

"Not once since our wedding," admitted Peggy.

"Oh, dear child. There are many, many women of your age who wish they could say that."

"You won't tell anyone, will you?"

Miss Carstairs tucked an arm beneath Peggy's elbow and kept her going. "Of course not. You can talk to me, Peggy, more closely than you would to your mother, if she were alive. I think any woman who lives with Constable Pinch needs another woman to talk to. Elfrida was always in my back garden, telling me things that she didn't want other people to hear. I thought our little private moments were making things safe, but not as it turned out. Only too late, did we learn how much matters had got on top of her."

"A sinner must be careful, for she might get what she wishes for. And I longed for Pinch badly. I prayed that I would marry him. Miss Carstairs, I take my vows very seriously. I know that it is my duty, before God, to obey my husband, and that means putting myself second."

"No woman would ask you to believe otherwise, Peggy."

"My problems amount to very little. Pinch is Pinch, of course, and perhaps that's all there is to it."

"I'm sure."

They had reached the vicarage gate. "How do you feel?" Miss Carstairs asked.

"Do you know, I feel very good about myself. Doing a mess on Edna Thurrock is the best thing I have ever done. It was well worth whatever I get for it." Peggy took a hanky from the cuff of her dress. "I'm fine. My nose is a little sniffly, that's all. Fine, really."

"Then you won't need me to come any further with you. I remember, in class three, when you dried painting brushes on Betty Drop's new apron. I told you off but you were so spirited, so determined not to explain and just as sure that you were right. In the end, I gave you the stick only because I knew it would put even more fire in your belly. But Peggy." She took hold of Peg's shivering hand before parting. "Not too much, hey?"

The bishop had decided that a vicar's den was the best indicator of his efforts for the parish. He held this truth to be so incontrovertible that every man who went visiting on his behalf obeyed instructions and poked their noses into the vicarage studies. He argued – because bishops are able to argue unreasonably – that a good study has French windows and a substantial hearth. He used to insist that something to do with fishes should be on the wall, because no man can be a sufficient student of human nature if he has not fished from wet river banks, but the bishop had recently been forced to accept that there was a modern breed of vicars who did not like to sit in the cold. "In which cases," he allowed, "their studies should be blessed with worthy chaos."

Alexander Beamish liked to fish and kept an untidy den, so he scored well. He had been taught that thorough preparation was the foundation of proper priestly practice. Now that he was sixty, he pooh-poohed the notion that sitting in a study for hours prepared a man for anything. "I have found that yesterday prepares us best for tomorrow," he had once said to the bishop. "One needs a place for reflection, that is all." The bishop, being seventy, chose not to argue. But Beamish's study was also a space for learning. Serious books filled two bookcases while half a dozen sensational novels sat, waiting, in different places. A well thumbed pile of scores lodged in a basket by the fireplace. Beamish couldn't sing and there wasn't a piano in the house, but he was one of those happy men who could be transported by the pleasure of reading music in silence. The dace in a glass case above the mantelpiece wasn't one of Beamish's trophies; it had been caught by his predecessor and Beamish wanted it to stay because no vicar should ever leave his vicarage completely.

But there were also times, as was now the case, when the vicar's study became the place to put things right. Tea in the drawing room might be a better option when reconciliation is sought between two parishioners but where there was only one miscreant, then it was proper that the wayward figure should be brought up to stand before the vicar's desk in the vicar's study.

Mrs Pinch tried to think that she was small and shy and not very strong. If she pictured it hard enough, perhaps the vicar would be deceived and not be too hard on her. God, she couldn't believe that she was standing in front of the vicar for a telling off. Was she in Jane Eyre or Oliver Twist, she wondered. She wanted to protest; she'd do better in Moll Flanders or that new book that Muriel had given her. But Mrs Pinch knew that it was always best to play according to the man's rules. Thank goodness that she had changed into uncomfortable shoes. Now, she could wince when they squeezed her toes, and the vicar would like a wince on her face. She shifted so that she was a bit pigeon-toed, held her hands together over her tummy and pretended that she didn't have the nerve to look him in the face.

The vicar was a tall man, given to wearing jackets and trousers that didn't match. He often chose shoes, Peggy noticed, which had been made to walk in other places. Golf shoes, hiking boots, black shoes where brown would have looked more comfortable, even wellingtons indoors. Peggy had decided, during one particularly turgid lecture from the pulpit, this footwear waywardness was because he was used to trampling on things. He had a head of tight brown curls, thick and wiry, which – Peggy had mused on a similar occasion – would frizzle in a second when he knelt too close to a fire, one day.

"This is nonsense," he said, slapping his hands down and pushing himself away from the desk. "What can I say to you that you don't already know?"

"I know it was wrong, Vicar. I'm very sorry." (She said this a little too primly.)

"Then you will say so to poor Edna," he said and started to pace up and down his pacing-up-and-down-rug.

"I can't do that."

"Why ever not?"

"Because then I'd have to do it to her again, Vicar. To make up for saying sorry."

He went to the end of the room, dropped onto a couch and masked his eyes with his hand. "You mean, she deserved it?" He sighed and leaned back so that he could view the paddock and orchard that extended from the study window to the churchyard wall. His parishioners were proud that the vicarage garden was the best in the village. People were always ready to plant and tender but, although Polly the maid, made good use of the kitchen plot, the rest of it was, oh, too private, too empty of people. Good things in the village are just too shut away, he reflected and returned his attention to Peggy Pinch. "I can't spend long on this," he said. "I've a young man polishing silver in the room next door. I can't tell you who, but I need to see to him."

"It's Ernest Berkeley, Vicar. I can hear him singing."

"I despair, I really do. You won't believe what I caught him doing in the middle of the night. 'Deal with him, father!' his parents say. How many times have I told them, we are Church of England, I've said. Not 'father' at all." He raised his hand in the air. "Deal with him, father! Well, a good poacher will never go hungry, I suppose. But the lad is rising eighteen. I mean, old enough for Pinch to deal with, never mind 'father'. What do I do? It's all part of our sickness. No, no. I can't tell you what he's done but he's polishing silver to make up for it." He shrugged. "Hardly enough. I mean, you and I know that. What good will it do?"

"It's a pity about the silver, Vicar," Peggy said. "I could have done that. Would you like me to chop wood instead? I was thinking, I could change into my corduroys and come back after tea."

"Oh, Peggy ," he sighed, worried and weary.

"I think, Vicar, don't you," said Peggy, looking around for a chair, "that 'Mrs Pinch' would be better."

"Oh yes, yes. I'm sure you're right. There's much that troubles me. It seems so many in our modest congregation take the presence of God too lightly. Something unholy is going on at Thorrucks Farm – I don't know what – but this morning the policeman's wife poured slops over the head of the farmer's wife, so the argument seems sufficiently well-cooked to be served beneath all our noses. Before lunch, I shall beat the Boy Berkeley for getting into mischief. Poor, dear, Lady Anne – her squire has been murdered. And then there is the matter of the shoolma'am's cat."

"The cat? Miss Carstairs' Queen o' Scots?"

"Oh yes, and a very curious affair, it is. Count the people who were out of doors on Sunday night, looking for her. It seems that the spinster's puss was a very convenient excuse for many of us to be away from our beds."

He paused and Peggy said, "I see," hoping she would be invited to sit down.

"Oh, further. I've had a visit from the bishop over the Corquet murder. Oh, enough is enough."

The clock on the mantelpiece slipped a gear, then chimed with a single 'ting' that sounded more like a Christmas toy than an expensive clock in a parson's parlour.

One o'clock. Pinch would have taken reports of her behaviour. Poisonous Miss Hestey would have been first: 'Disgraced her mother's memory, that's what I say. It's only fair that I tell you everything that happened, from beginning to end, Mr Pinch.' From the postmistress: 'I want to know what made a wife do that.' (This, just too loud to be behind his back.) 'Farmer Thurrock has every right to complain to your superior. No, we must, all of us, insist upon a proper enquiry.' 'That's what you get from leaving the doors open.' Miss Carstairs would have said nothing but, no doubt, she planned to make the policeman a cup of tea later in the week.

Peggy knew that she had hurt him. She had embarrassed him in front of his public. By now, he would have withdrawn to a private hidey-hole where he could battle with the turmoil of his emotions. He could never understand his feelings, Peggy knew that. He could never separate the raisins and custard from the gorge of pudding coming up from his pork belly. Pinch would put his head to the wind and endure the storm. When he emerged from his hour of purgatory, he would be sure that he needed to respond. He must do something about it. And, from the first moments of her naughty idea, Peggy knew what that would be.

"Do you have to stand there like that?" the vicar was saying. "Can't you sit in one of the chairs?"

She sat down. "The bishop, Vicar? You were saying."

"Yes, er ..."

"... Mrs Pinch?"

"Yes, Mrs Pinch. The bishop has called on me. With this General Strike – he's sure that it will go ahead – it seems that there's a nervousness that old Corker's death could be part of something much deeper."

"I know. Pinch had a similar visit from Scotland Yard. Can you imagine anyone asking Pinch for advice?" Her hand went to her mouth. "Oh, how awful of me. I don't know what made me say that."

"Mrs Pinch, please do stop acting and I'd rather you sit properly."

Peg felt caught out. She was sure that she hadn't been showing too much of herself or making too much of her shapeliness. She checked her hair; it was decently tucked beneath her cloche hat. Yes, she had been thinking like a cocky child, but that was because she knew she was in trouble and wanted to build herself up. Being told off by the vicar had been inevitable; she would also have to put up with whispers and tut-tutting for a couple of weeks. Behaving like a tough nut, who knew her own mind, was just part of getting ready for that. She knew that even when she had dealt with these things, she still had to make amends to the people she had let down. Like Pinch. Like Miss Carstairs and Muriel on the bus. But surely –

she checked her hair again and patted the lap of her dress – she hadn't let too much of her bravado show.

"And, oh." The vicar was shaking his bowed head. "Is it my place to worry about the Major's locomotive?"

"Locomotive, Vicar?"

"Oh yes, locomotive, Mrs Pinch. The Major showed me his toy train last week, and it seemed exactly the same as the one that went missing from Harry Thurrock's barn last Whitsuntide."

"Toy train, Vicar? I can't believe anyone would kill anyone else because of a toy train. I shouldn't worry about that, Vicar."

"Peggy, where was your husband last Sunday night? I'm sorry but I have to ask you about Mr Pinch and his whereabouts."

"Then you'd do better asking the man himself, rather than pressing his wife to tell stories."

"Peggy ..."

"Mrs Pinch."

"Peggy," insisted the vicar. "I have known you since you were a young child who scampered out of my church whenever a sermon started. You are an honest woman, who works hard for our parish, but there are times when you use your allegiance to duty as a shield rather than a spear. Cleanliness may be next to godliness but it shouldn't excuse us from pulling up the stubborn weeds."

The vicar's pulpit was making her eyelids heavy. Peggy always struggled to pay attention.

"A murder has been done in our village," he said. "It is not my calling to catch the culprit, nor even to call him to account. But I cannot stand by while rumour and loose talk do their worst. Your husband is very popular in this village. You should be proud of him. I know that a great many women in the parish are grateful for his service."

Peggy sat up but let the remark pass. At least, she was re-assured that the vicar had no suspicion about their arrangement with the Thurrock couple. Otherwise, he would not have made such a clumsy faux-pas.

"Mr Pinch has a happy way of being where people expect to find him," the vicar said. "If he patrols after dark, a man can always find him outside our church gate at midnight. I, myself, have shared many of these happy moments with him, smoking our pipes as we watch the last few houselamps go out, one by one. Now, we know that Pinch was out and about last Sunday night. Boy Berkeley saw him making a call from the Red Lion's lobby at nine, and he walked Miss Hestey home after one o'clock. No-one saw him in between."

The vicar shook his head. "He wasn't at the church gate at midnight. What was he up to?"

Peggy collected her thoughts. "There really is no puzzle, Vicar. I was at my garden gate at twelve o'clock. I didn't see Pinch, but I didn't see you either, and if you tell me that he was walking Miss Hestey home, then that is explanation enough."

"But why would he make a call from the Lion, when there is a private phone – free of charge, I believe – in the Police House, not one hundred yards away?"

"Vicar, if you are trying to tell me that my husband made a telephone call in the village pub so that I wouldn't hear it, then it's my business not to know about it."

"Does it bother you that Jessica is still in the parish?" he asked quickly.

"No, of course not. I like Jessica very much."

"Then, I'm sure she'd like to feel such friendship."

"Has she spoken to you?"

Beamish dipped his head. "I'm sure she'd welcome more time with you."

So, Pinch's daughter had confided in the vicar. And now, Peggy felt selfish. Jessica and Peggy were only two years apart and, because each had lost their mother, they should have been able to share so much, but Peggy couldn't dismiss a feeling that her marriage to Pinch had stolen his daughter's chance to be close to her only parent. Sometimes, Jessica spoke as if she hated her dad, and Peggy feared that she should take the blame for that as well. She stayed away from the woman. Was she nervous that she and Jessica might talk too much? Life with Pinch wasn't easy and sometimes Peggy had to draw on every ounce of her loyalty to keep going. If she and Jessica became true friends, if they became sisters (as they ought to have been), Larksteer Cottage might be too ready a refuge on difficult days. All that was true, but Peggy was aware of a greater truth: the women shared the loss of a mother, Peggy didn't want to share Pinch as well.

"Sometimes," she said, her voice quiet and croaky. "I find that I have to do things I'm not proud of."

"Of course," said the vicar with an understanding which Peg almost resented. "That is part of living under the sun."

"I shall stay behind after Church on Sunday so that everyone can see me. They'll all walk past my pew and they'll know that I'm in detention. They'll like that."

"Yes," he conceded wearily. "I'm afraid many people in our village would like that very much." The vicar had the look of a worried man. As he sat on the couch, he kept pressing his fingers to his forehead as if to concentrate a frown, and his legs couldn't be still. He crossed and uncrossed his ankles, he folded one knee over the other, he stretched, he poked his toes inwards and outwards. Things were on his mind that needed running off. "When I first visited the parish and it was still in the care of my predecessor, I was appalled to find the old scold's bridle displayed in the nave. I promised that it would be removed as soon as I took up the living. But it's still there, you note. It hangs as a warning to the wicked tongues and eager ears amongst us."

"You mean the Hestey woman?"

"Oh yes, Miss Hestey. Let's mark her. Everyone has her labelled as the village scold. Not quite a witch; after all, these are enlightened times, Mrs Pinch. Well, I'll tell you. Hestey was the woman who searched longest for Queen O' Scots. The longest and the most thoroughly. Oh, I know she has a careless mouth. Yes, Miss Hestey would do well to stand before the artefact and construct the experience of suffering the bridle's discomfort. But many more in our parish carry Miss Hestey's mischief in their hearts. Are they not as guilty?"

Peggy's response was unexpected. "It's never been used," she said. "It has been pegged to the stonework throughout my life . As children we used to scare one another with stories of torture and mutilation and death by choking. It's a measure of man's cruelty to woman, Vicar."

"A reminder, you mean?"

"A statement, I think. It says, this is what we can do to you. It's an evil that has no place in our church."

The vicar's face had turned as stern, and as horrible, as she had seen it.

"There are moments, Peggy Pinch, when I fear you might be a rather dangerous thing. Yes, I think it would be helpful if you chopped wood in the vicarage garden. But not this evening. I think it's important that people see you walking up the village street, on your way to do the work. Shall we say, half past seven in the morning, and be suitably dressed for heavy toil? I think a little public humility will do Mrs Pinch no harm. Half past seven until half past ten. Now, how much wood is appropriate for three hours labour? I mean, fairly rigorous labour, I think. Anything less would hardly fit the bill. I shall ask the kitchen maid to ensure that a sufficient load is stacked behind the woodshed. I've always found her to be a good judge in these matters. There's poetry in it, don't you think? A lowly maid from a hovel in Wretched Lane, deciding the punishment for the policeman's wife."

He paused.

"Or, would it be better?" he continued. "Yes, I shall ask Edna Thurrock to decide how high the pile of logs should be."

Peggy Pinch felt her eyes fill. "Please don't," she said. "Please ..." I hate her, she wanted to say. She swallowed, forcing back the tears. "Please don't do that."

Pinch came in at three. He changed into his gardening trousers and kept himself occupied for the rest of the day so that he wouldn't have to listen. Peg worked at her sink, watching her husband through the scullery window. "I did it because I was jealous," she muttered. "She does things with you that we don't. She says things to you that we can't speak about. And I'm angry."

She brought her mother's scrapbook from the larder shelf and, following a Victorian recipe, gathered the ingredients for tomorrow's cookery. "Angry, because she's stopping me getting to close you and ..." Peg wanted to break off, because the words were beginning to choke her but, of course, they kept coming. "And she's got that closeness and turned it into something bad. She has what I haven't and she's thrown it away."

She set the pots and wrapped pats of fat on the kitchen table and went back to the window. "I know what I've done to you." She wanted to shout at him: "I do know how you feel!" From the day that he had proposed, Pinch had conceded that a man who marries a lass from a younger generation must be prepared for embarrassment and humilitation at times. Folk had warned him that he wasn't the man to tame a spirited girl like Peggy. "I've given them a reason to say, 'We told you so.' I put the words in their mouths, I know. I know."

She knew that Pinch would be stopping soon for a smoke of his pipe. She put the kettle on the stove.

"I love you, Pinch," she said to herself, "and don't I honour you? Don't I take second place whenever you talk? I won't have a word said against you. And ..." She felt the words getting the better of her again. "My God, I'm desperate to obey. But God alone knows what you want me to do because, Mr Pinch, there are days when I certainly do not!" She let things simmer. "I want to be a good wife. And dutiful, I want to be a dutiful wife."

But it all meant nothing while Peg was in the kitchen and Pinch was in the garden.

He didn't look at her when she carried the tea to the little bird-table. She nearly asked, 'Can I tell you why?' but she knew that he would reply 'The question is not to be spoken of.'

At nine o'clock, Peg was undressing in the kitchen. Her patterned nightdress, with its high collar, buttoned cuffs and embroidered bodice was due for the laundry basket but she would wear it for one more night. Because it was the warmest nightie she had and because even a fresh nightie would be especially grubby before morning. She had boiled a pot of rich cocoa and poured a large portion for herself into a clay jug. She placed a saucer on top so that it wouldn't cool before Pinch came in from the garden.

He worked until the light faded. It was black and chilly outside, and a quarrelsome wind rattled cottage doors, up and down the village street. Peg knew that Pinch had a half completed jigsaw on the parlour table and, more than anything at this moment, she wanted to help him finish it. Peggy carried a ball of two socks in her left hand; she wouldn't put them on until she was in bed (keeping them clean). The stone flags of the scullery floor were spitefully cold to her feet. She closed her eyes; she wasn't near tears but she needed to settle a tremor of nerves.

"Pinch, I want to explain," she said when she heard him scraping his boots. She nearly said, 'it's only fair' but her conscience checked her. She believed that Pinch had been very fair, very reasonable (and Edna Thurrock had been very deserving).

"I have said that the question shall never be discussed," he said, even tempered.

Husband and wife stood face to face. He was serious and sombre but not stern. His pale blue eyes – which could be so readily disconcerting when he was in a truculent mood – showed no hint of malice or cruel satisfaction. Peggy saw a wise and kind man, close to God and deserving sympathy. Her prank had shamed him throughout the village, yet he hadn't struck her, he hadn't berated her. But he had resolved to put matters right with a sore lesson for her. Last night, on the back step, her naughty idea had seemed worth this inevitable punishment but, now that it was close, wasn't there some way back?

"It gets so cold in the middle of the night," was the only plea she offered. She collected the jug of cocoa and followed her husband down the three steps and along the short passage to the open cell door. An army blanket had been folded to provide a mattress on the stone bed and she was allowed two others. There was a chamber pot and nothing else. She hesitated; she couldn't argue that she hadn't earned this discomfort but, oh, how she hated it. "The cold, Pinch. Please, I won't be able to take it." There was nothing more to say. She stepped inside and immediately sat on the blankets so that she could put the bedsocks on. From now on, keeping warm was the only thing that mattered.

He slammed the cell door. Metal worked against metal as he screwed the key in the lock. He banged two extra bolts home. Then he made deliberately heavy footsteps as he retreated along the passage. He heard her call, "Good night, my love," as he locked the door to the kitchen. Pinch didn't reply.

CHAPTER FOUR

At midnight, the Thurrocks were in each other's arms on the wooden veranda of their farmhouse. Harry was sitting forward in an old captain's chair and his wife sat contentedly at his feet. She was reaching up to make sure that his long arms stayed wrapped around her bust. They were wearing working clothes and had been busy until forty-five minutes ago. A small bonfire, not twenty feet from the house, cast a hot glow across their faces and the wind, which was such a nuisance in the village, kept the smoke and fiery flecks out of their hair.

"Every time was horrible," she said. "He was vulgar and dirty. And he was rude, Harry."

"You should have said." His finger was curling a lock of her hair.

"Do you remember when we spoke about the stock that we wanted for our son?"

"They were silly conversations, Ed. Nothing more. Didn't we say a long nose and stout bandy legs?"

"You might have done!" laughed Edna. "I certainly didn't."

"But you did, you did," he teased, wanting to lighten her talk.

"Then you must have got me merry first. No, I remember powerful, reliable and strong."

"Godfearing," said Harry.

"And just."

"Yes, we agreed that PC Pinch was always fair with people. He had the wisdom of years."

"Yes, he was all these things but he was also dirty. A ruffian."

"Why didn't you tell me. I would have stopped it all at once."

"Of course you would, and that's why I didn't. Besides, he never hurt me. But I always knew that I'd be a fool to cross him. That's why I didn't tell you at once. That's why, on that last afternoon, once he was here, expecting to enjoy me ..."

"Edna, you don't have to explain anything to me. I know that I played the easy part. All I had to do was stand by. Good Lord, I would never judge you for anything you did." He said, "I don't know how I would have felt if you had enjoyed his attentions."

"Oh Harry, he was coarse mustard while you are sweet cranberry."

"Then let's say no more."

But Edna added, "He trumpeted in bed."

"Edna!" Thurrock laughed loudly. "Please spare me!"

"And he touched himself."

"Edna, you're scandalous!"

"But he did, all the time, like a lad who had grown up on his own."

They both laughed and clapped their hands. "Like the Boy Berkeley!" they shouted together.

Ernie 'Boy' Berkeley's eyes peered out from the blackness of the barn. He giggled at the sound of his name; the laugh was on them. He had done his devilment, now he had nothing to do but wait. Being trapped in the hayloft made the lark even better because he could not have been awarded a better view of the entertainment. The money had not been disturbed. He had hidden it months ago. He took out only a few shillings at a time and sometimes added more in a week than he spent. He was sure that the shotgun would never be discovered, wrapped in its leather blanket and wedged between the old casks. He had found the gun only an hour after the shooting of Major Corquet when Tom Hall was tramping across the heath and before the soldiers arrived. Only the curiosity of PC Pinch had prevented Berkeley searching Holt's Crossing properly and removing all the clues. The village bobby had spent forty minutes walking up and down the railway lines, sometimes bending down to examine possible evidence and sometimes stepping away from the track so that he could assess the lie of the bed. But, when Pinch's back was turned, Berkeley recovered the murder weapon with no trouble. The culprit had tossed it into long grass, a few yards from the lineside sheds. Pinch was a bimbo to have missed it.

"I'm streets ahead," he muttered as the Thurrocks joked on their porch. A silly pair, he thought and wriggled as he pictured what was to come. "They have hardly started investigatin' and I know nearly all that there is to know."

The farmer's wife was cold now and wanted to go in but Mister called her a spoil-sport; he wanted to kneel at her feet and say his poems. Rain would make it even funnier, Berkeley mused, but there was no chance of that.

Two things were going on in Berkeley's head. He was thinking excitedly about Mr and Mrs Thurrock while words about the murder kept bubbling into his mouth. At times like this, Berkeley thought that he was two people, Boy Berkeley himself and Boy Berkeley inside.

"I'll let the police know bit by bit," he whispered. "So that Pinch makes a fool of himself."

The Thurrocks were still laughing. By now, Edna was sitting against the wooden slatwork of their front wall and Harry was prancing along the veranda like an entertainer. The farmyard was quiet. If Berkeley listened hard, he could occasionally hear the water move in the duckpond but the animals made no sound, and the wind was too light to push against the barn doors and window shutters. The night was so quiet that the clanking of the midnight train sounded clearly across the landscape. The single light on the engine flickered far off but Berkeley recognised the nose of a small tank loco pulling a light load. It stopped about two hundred yards from Holt's Crossing – three miles from the farm – and waited, its boiler panting and the brakes and shafts moaning like a beast in harness.

Harry Thurrock heard it too and looked out from the edge of the veranda. "There's been night traffic every night this week and it's not usual. Lady Anne says the Major was expecting army transports in case of the emergency but I'd like to know what and to where. A fellow needs to know about his neck of the woods. We're in a sorry state, Edna. Guns across our countryside. Trains under guard. People say they'll put tanks into the docks if the strike goes ahead. Whoever's heard of it; tanks on the streets of England?"

"Verger Meggastones was talking in the village," Edna said. "He says that the Major knew all about the freight train coming through. His steward's a sergeant in the reserves and was part of the detail."

"In which case he shouldn't be talking about it."

"Well, he didn't need to. I heard Verger Meggastones talking to Miss Hestey, I said, who had got it from the laundry maid at Home Farm, who'd put two and two together having seen the state of Steward Orton's uniform."

"So, why is Miss Hestey interested?" Harry asked.

"Because, she is. You know she is. She's always interested in anything about Steward Orton. They used to be sweethearts, didn't they?"

"Oh, that was years ago. It was a boy and girl thing. There's been nothing between them since the war."

"So you say." Edna drew breath, "Harry, you're not worrying about the Black Prince, are you?"

"I give it no mind, these days," he replied.

"It was beautiful," Edna reflected.

"It was finely done, though I say so myself, but the thing was cursed from the start. It brought foul jealousy and dark conspiracy. It made the worst of men. Like the richest diamond or a king's treasure, no man could lay his eye on it and not want to own it. The bad boy stole it. You say that and I say it. But it will do him no good. One day he'll be caught and when that happens, I hope he'll be called to answer for greater wrongs than the theft of a toy train."

"Let's put Berkeley out of our minds. Harry, it's chilly for me. I'm going in." But when she tried to get to her feet, she complained, "The skirt of my dress, Harold, it's caught in the door."

"It can't be," he said as he came to her aid. "God, Edna. What's this about? What's happened here? Hey, the door's locked from the inside."

Berkeley pressed his hands between his legs; it was the only way he could hold back the giggles. He watched the man run round to the back of the house, just as he knew he would do, and when he came back, shouting, "We're locked out, Ed. Locked out of our own home," Berkeley thrilled with mischievous delight.

"We know you're out there! We know it's you!" Harry Thurrock was standing on the top of the veranda steps, shaking his fist. "I don't know where you are and you'll not get me to come searching for you. Berkeley, I'll shoot your head from your neck one of these days."

"Please, Harry. Try the windows."

"A waste of time. He'll have bolted those. He knows we'll have to force our way in." He stamped his feet with frustration, then gave in to impulse and ran forward across the dirt yard. "Berekeley! Berkeley, I'm going to get you!"

But, oh, the lock-out was just the start of the rascal's mischief.

"Harry!" shouted the farmer's wife. "The pen's open. Harry, quick. The pigs are out!"

Harry braked, slipped down to one knee, recovered in seconds and, cursing Berkeley loudly, ran around the barn to deal with the liberated pigs. But his shouting had spooked the animals and there was soon a cocophony of oinking, snorting, and trotters in wet mud.

Edna was still tethered to the door. "I'm coming, Harry," she called. For a few seconds she considered ripping her dress free but by kneeling, then crouching, then lying down, she managed to haul the dress over her head. Lifting her cotton slip to her thighs, she jumped from the veranda and ran after her husband. The mud soon dirtied her legs and underwear.

"Hold back, hold back." Thurrock had swung out his arm, like a policeman stopping the traffic behind him. "Chasing's no good," he said, his farmyard sense having caught up with him at last. "If we're to catch these blighters, we're got to think like them."

"That's right, Thurrock," whispered Berkeley. "Think like smelly pigs." He had decamped from the barn and was hiding in the weeds and rough stalks at the swampy end of a duck pond, fifty yards from the couple. So far, everything had gone to plan. He wrapped the rope's end around his knuckles, made himself flat, and waited.

"We need some lights!" shouted Edna. "Harry, I'll fetch some lights." She turned around and ran towards the barn, holding her shift higher than ever so that her fat thighs and hips wobbled white in the night.

Berkeley kept his free hand over his mouth, but he couldn't stop giggling down his nose. 'She's good with lights in the barn,' he was thinking. He remembered how, three months ago, she had laid out a bed of straw, lit it with lanterns and dressed it with flowers. She had stuck some of the flowers in her hair, which made her look stupid. A carthorse with daisies – something made up for fun.

Berkeley tested the strain on the rope, careful not to tug too hard. Everything was working well. But when the Thurrock woman came running from the barn, Harry and the pigs were too close to the house. If she ran towards them, she wouldn't spy Berkeley's hiding place, so the youth pushed himself above the reeds, just enough – and, yes, she caught sight of him.

"Get away from here!" she screamed, making for the duck pond now. "I told you never to come near again!"

"You can't catch me," he sang, standing up straight.

She didn't stop. In seconds, her heavy feet were slapping on the little wooden jetty. Berkeley waited until she was over the water, then pulled the rope. The jetty collapsed and Edna Thurrock splashed into the stagnant pool.

"Stand up, Edna!" Berkeley squealed. "Go on, you can stand up in the pond. Stand up and show off your lolloppers, all wet and dripping."

"You're in trouble now!" But she couldn't get the words out properly. She was choking and spitting, wiping the dirty water from her mouth. "Go! Please go!"

Berkeley was chuckling, holding his flies tight (pinching them, almost) and waggling his head on his shoulders. "You're fearing your husband might catch me, and I'll tell him too much as about you and me and that barn. Four times over, it was. And how proud you were, lying there in the hay with young Berkeley astride you. Remember the silly flowers in your hair, when your face was all a-glow? A young fox with a mighty brush. That's what you called me."

57

Thurrock had abandoned the pigs and was running for the duck pond.

"Please, Ernest. Please," said Edna, shaking her head. Water was up to her knees. Pond grass and sludge hung from her hair and shoulders. Still, she was holding her shift up, although everything was already sopping wet.

"But you can't have Boy Berkeley as the father of your pup, can you, Edna Thurrock? Not good enough, is he? How could you tell Farmer Thurrock as what you've been doing with a young lad, as half his age. God's snakes, you must have been right relieved when your old man gets an idea to put Pinch'em in his place. In your place, I mean." Berkeley laughed at his dirty joke. "In your place, in his place. Snakes, he can't begin to know how filthy you are. A filthy woman, that's what Peg Pinchie called you. You're a filthy, filthy woman, Edna Thurrock."

Berkeley waited until Thurrock was only feet from the landing, then he turned tail. He judged that the farmer would look after his sopping wife rather than chase him. He put twenty yards between them, then he waved back, shouting, "Boy Berkeley's in charge now. Boy Berkeley's the winner and he's going to make you all tell, just as you're like. Policeman Pinch and the fat whore Thurrock. And Tom Hall's wicked mind. Then Reverend Beamo and what he likes, and his Lady Anne who knows no better. Listen hard, you all. Boy Berkeley's going to make you learn!"

PART TWO

CHAPTER FIVE

PC Pinch sprang the cell lock at half past five but he was out of the house before his wife emerged. He had been early out of bed; the impending national emergency and the local murder made it likely that a supervising inspector would visit, so Pinch made sure that he booked himself 'on duty' in the register and signed for the official keys and petty cash before he went on patrol.

He walked to the little triangle of green at the top of the village, where The Street and Back Lane met in front of the churchyard gates, and surveyed his beat. Already, smoke was drifting from the one or two homes where early morning fires were lit (many of the neighbours would save their coal until they returned from their morning errands). Pinch thought that nothing was more beautiful than his village, waking early in the morning. Whatever the weather or time of year, the sounds of the first horses on the village street, the postman and the newspaper boy, the one or two car engines starting up and the unlatching of windows and doors reassured him that he was in the middle of something charming and permanent. Natural history played its part. The hedges and trees made different noises in different seasons. The everyday sightings of individual birds until he came to look upon them as comforting acquaintances, if not friends, made him think that the village was a safe and wise place in which to settle. Neither the murder of Major Corquet, nor Mrs Pinch's upsetting behaviour, nor even the threat of a national labour strike could dent that confidence. Whatever happened, the essential rightness of Pinch and his world would carry on unchallenged. Every year, he had seen the village work through bad weather – flooded ditches, fallen trees, snow drifts and days of being cut off and, always, Miss Hestey would talk too much, the Reverend Beamish would worriedly shake his head and the children would find important jobs to do.

Keeping to his country copper's pace, he crossed the road and followed a wooded track to the keeper's hut on the edge of the Corquet estate. Here, at half past six every morning, Jake Timothy shared a grace and favour breakfast with Pinch, Dale the gunsmith and old Mr Jones from Home Farm.

"I thought you would be missing like Monday," Jones growled over his fowl and black pudding, and Pinch was about to say that he'd allow no talk of Peggy's misconduct, when the old hand explained, "I thought you'd be entertaining the London detective."

"You've asked us no questions, Pinch," queried the gunsmith

"That's why he stayed at home for Monday's breakfast so that he could question Hestey-woman."

"Hestey-woman, as you call her, Jonesy, needs no questioning. She comes forth with her observations readily enough."

"Ah, so she does," Jones agreed. "And what about Tom Hall? I say he's run off Eastleigh way."

The keeper put four wooden beakers of ale on the table. "You're putting our Pinch in a corner. Leave police business alone, I say."

The talk settled on 'the emergency'. The Great Strike was inevitable; it would be called in the next three days, the men decided. Jones kept repeating that there were 'rights and wrongs in the matter' and there would be 'winners and losers' but Jones was not a man given to detailed argument. His conclusion sounded more like a plea: "We can't have a strike; it'll put ninepence on income tax." When the keeper pronounced 'desperate changes, reaching further than the fences,' Pinch thought that he was seeing the dispute as one part of a broader insurrection. But when he considered the comment, while Jones and the gunsmith were talking about the folly of 'stocking up', Pinch realised that Jake had been drawing conclusions from the murder at Holt's Crossing.

"You think Lady Anne will sell?" Pinched asked, cutting across others' conversation.

Jones came in quickly, "I've known that the Major's was the only voice against it."

The breakfast broke at seven-thirty – it never lingered – but as the gentlemen were leaving, the keeper caught hold of Pinch's tunic. "Wait on, Pinch-man, there's a matter I can't hold back from you, though her ladyship says I should."

Pinch gestured that he shouldn't speak further until the others were well clear. He looked at the weather-beaten face with long grey eyebrows and a mouth made lopsided by missing teeth.

"I can't account for one of the guns in here," continued the gamekeeper. "I've determined that it went missing on the night of the murder. Lady Anne says I should keep quiet, that it will turn up like all the guns that go missing on the estate. But I can't think it's right to hold back such intelligence when a murder's been done."

"Who has access to the cupboards here?" asked Pinch.

"The keys are kept in the gunroom in the old Manor House, so anyone on the estate could lay their hands on them. I've got my own set, of course, as had the Major. And I know that Berkeley Boy gets in here when it's locked, though I can't see how."

"Were you about during that night?"

"That's my job, Pinch-man."

"Then you can tell us just when the shotgun went missing."

"O.K. Later than twenty to twelve and sooner than quarter past."

Pinch nodded. "I can't ask you any more. The man from Scotland Yard is investgating. I'll tell him you need to speak to him."

"Watch your back with that Inspector York. He's after your hide. He was asking Hestey-woman, last night, if you had ever done anything wrong that he ought to know about. She said she'd go off and think about it, so you tread carefully, eh? As for my missing gun, you tell him what you know, but you can't say where from. I got my job to think about, Pinch-man. That's why I've told you and no-one else."

PC Pinch agreed to the compact and, leaving the keeper in his shed, walked along the rough track of Wretched Lane, away from the village, to the boundary of Thurrock's top field. There, for forty minutes, he tried again to answer the question that had puzzled him at the Idling Pool, two days before. He thought of the routes that Major Corquet could have taken from the Old Manor House to Holt's Crossing, he tried to work out what could be seen from the middle thicket and he asked how long it would take a man to cross the heath to Larksteer Cottage.

He was still there when Reverend Beamish took up a place at the fence. "You're worried about the geography," he said.

Pinch explained. "There are only three places that count. Thurrock's Farm, the old Manor House, and Larksteer Cottage. There is Home Farm, yes, and the buildings that make up Manor Farm, but they are too far away to bother us. I suppose, properly, we should add the village and Wretched Lane to the map. If you draw the paths that a man would take between those places, he has no reason to pass Holt's Crossing. The crossing is there so that a horse can go from one side of the line to the other, avoiding the soft ground on the edge of the moor."

"This worries you?" the vicar asked uneasily.

"I am trying to give a man a reason for being there. But there's no other answer to it. Harry Thurrock did this thing and he'll be necked for it." Pinch gave a long sigh. "There will be distressed sales of two farmsteads inside a twelvemonth. They'll fetch no price. Believe me, Vicar, many of us should fret about our livings."

Reverend Beamish looked like a man who was already worried about his.

"You're flumoxed, Beamish. You don't know what to say."

"Pinch," he began, having cleared his throat and tugged at his ear. "I must talk to you about dear Peggity. I sometimes suspect that she carries some quite radical thoughts in her silly head. Quite dangerous thoughts, I fear. I'm sure we would want you to guide her."

Pinch, still looking across the vale of countryside, laughed lightly. "Ah now, Vicar. That's my problem."

"Pardon? I mean, if I can help in any ..."

"The cigarettes."

"Cigarettes?"

64

"Oh, yes. Cigarettes. When I vowed at her mother's death bed to look after the little Peg, I had already fallen in love with the girl. I had caught her watching me chop wood one day at the edge of Holt's Ridge. That's the first time I saw her. I think I sensed, even then, that she'd be more than I could control."

"Ah, I see. Yes, very warming. But, cigarettes?"

Pinch nodded. "Peggy started to smoke only a few weeks after our wedding. I said that her mother wouldn't like to see it, so Peggy stopped. She is a very good girl. A dutiful daughter and an obedient wife."

"Well, that is ..."

"Within a month, I was shown the worst of womanly moods. I felt that I had married a barking, tearful, silent, snappy whippet – I have to say, Vicar, I thanked God when she gave in to sin and went back to her cigarettes."

"If I can help, Pinch, in any ..."

"The trouble, Beamish, is that when I see my wife smoking, I see the woman I love. That makes me unfaithful to the promise I gave her mother. Am I a husband or a guardian? I am twenty-six years her senior, remember."

"Well, now ..."

"I have prayed."

"Ah! Good!"

"And after my prayers, I can see clearly that my duty is to her mother. My promise to take care of Peggy, and to guide her, comes first. Which means, of course, that my wife cannot stand the sight of me."

Pinch changed the subject. "The Constabulary regrets that we will receive no extra delivery of coal before the strike. Vital stations will be provisioned but not country Police Houses. I think they mean 'crucial' for if we are not vital, we must be dead." After a moment's reflection, he added, "It may be that they mean vital, after all. However, because of the murder of Major Corquet, I am not required to present myself at a city division for special duties during the emergency. I am allowed to rest in peace, peacefully, so some good appears to have come from Inspector York's interference. He is not a real policeman, by the way; he is too short." Pinch walked away. His breakfast was not digesting well, and he wanted to be without company when his stomach sorted it out.

Peg had never seen the vicarage gardens and expected to work alone for three hours with The Street out of sight and the garden shed hiding her from the vicarage windows. She had brought her cigarettes and, before she started, sat on her allocated pile of wood and smoked. That's when she realised, uneasily, that the church was only three hundred yards away, on higher ground, and anyone at St Stephen's porch would have a clear view of her. No sooner had she come to terms with her lost privacy than the postman cut through the garden on his way to the poor cottages on the unmade track. Then Harry Thurrock's nephew parked his cart at the front of the house and came across the grass with a jug of fresh milk, explaining that he always took his rest in the vicarage garden before completing the second half of his round. "Uncle H doesn't know," he said. "Or I guess he does. Someone will have told him by now. You'd think you could be on your own in a vicar's garden, wouldn't you?"

She was about to start work when Polly Gunn trotted up. The young girl with frizzy hair and scraped ankles wore blue and grey at work. She tried to look like a nurse because she didn't want people to think that she was only a kitchen maid. Working for the vicar, she often said to herself, was working for a gentleman who lived alone, and that made her something that other helps weren't.

"Everyone gets a glass of lemonade at eleven o'clock and you won't be left out."

Peggy smiled, said thank you and picked up the chopper, but the maid dithered.

"You mustn't think bad of Reverend."

"I don't feel bad at all."

She thought that the maid was looking at her in a funny way and became uncomfortably conscious that she was wearing someone else's clothes. The stable jacket with leather shoulders and the baggy

66

corduroys, held up with braces, had been left in the bicycle shed by the Police House's previous couple.

"But you must be sore."

"No, really. A little humility will do me good. I realise now that I was very silly to do what I did and chopping wood will make amends."

Peggy could tell that young Polly wanted to fiddle with her hair and sort out her waist. Those fidgets got displaced to her toes, which pinched and squeezed until Polly was tottering like a doll on a spindle.

"Reverend is so kind, and what he did was only his obligations."

"Obligations?" queried Peggy. "Whatever did he do?"

"His duty, then. You mustn't think all men are bad."

Still, the girl wouldn't walk away. "He came round my house last night and said I was to make sure that the woodstack was high enough. He told me what had gone on and what you had to do about it."

"That was very good of him," said Peggy.

"At first I thought he was rude, coming round to a young girl's home when he knows her mother's in Bolton."

"Bolton?"

"Because my grandad went to the Final Tie and had his head taken off, so mother's gone to look after him."

"My, my. His head taken off?"

"As good as, mother says. Her postcard calls it a proper vinegar and brown paper job. That's why the Reverend thought I'd be better kept busy. Being on my own."

"I'm sure."

"I came out especially, last night, and shouted across the gardens for Ernest Berkeley to come at once. 'Come here, young Master Berkeley and sort out Mrs Pinch's punishment,' I shouted."

"And that was very good of you, too."

"As loud as I could."

"I'm sure."

"I said he had to build up the log pile. I had to do that, Mrs Pinch, or it wouldn't have been fair."

Peggy dipped her head and, if she had been wearing spectacles, she would have been peering over them.

"I said he had to make sure there was some knotty ones, otherwise they split too easily and you wouldn't have to work at it."

"Eleven o'clock, then," Peggy said.

"Mrs Pinch?"

"The lemonade, Polly."

"Yes." The girl took a step backwards. "Yes, Mrs Pinch."

"And you won't be looking, will you?"

"Of course not, Mrs Pinch. What do you take me for? Although the vicar did say that if you didn't chop all the logs, every one of them, we couldn't consider the job done."

"My, hasn't he had a lot to say?"

At last, the maid walked back to the house. Peggy told herself that she was wrong to wonder how the girl would look with potato slop dripping from her hair.

She got ready to split her first log. 'You mustn't think all men are bad?' Did she mean that Pinch was bad and Peggy shouldn't judge other men in the same way? Really? Did the whole village think that Pinch was cruel to her?

Peggy was soon into the swing of it. She enjoyed hard work and thought that she might make a regular chore of chopping the vicar's wood. Then she remembered that her effort was supposed to be a punishment so she slowed down for a few minutes and tried to make a drudge of it. But Peg couldn't work in a monotonous slog; she had to go fast and rest, fast and rest. It was a quarter to ten before she realised that Queen O'Scots had settled on the woodshed roof, the graveyard donkey had propped her head over the flint wall, twenty yards away, and Mr Carter's goats had stolen their way into the vicar's orchard (Peg was sure that someone ought to do something about that).

She was smoking her second cigarette, cross-legged on the rough grass, when the Boy Berkeley appeared from the vicar's row of fruit trees.

"I want to talk with you," he said.

"Then let's go in the shed where no-one can see us."

Peggy couldn't make up her mind about him. Some people said that he was fourteen, others that he was seventeen but acted younger. Sometimes, Peggy thought he was a sharp thinker and much older than he pretended. He wore a waistcoat of rabbit pelts and a pair of rough trousers that almost reached his chest. They were tied with string. He had some yellow grass in his mouth, he kept his hands in his pockets and mumbled to himself as he followed Peggy into the little hut.

"You've saved my life, Mrs Pinch," he insisted. "I've got to thank you for that. If you hadn't been at the vicarage yesterday morning, I reckon I'd have got my throat cut by now."

"Heavens," said Peggy, knowing that young men saw drama in everything. "Pirates?"

"Murderers, I'm sure."

Peggy didn't ask for further explanation but Berkeley, moving the straw from one corner of his mouth to the other, carried on without prompting. "This affair says nothing will pass unnoticed."

"Oh, Ernest, enough. You make a dreadful actor. Now, stop."

"Yesterday, our vicar was giving me a hiding in his study. Miss Hestey heard the commotion from the church path and, when she saw you leave the vicarage by the back door, she thought that it must have been you."

Peggy smiled. "Now, why would I be giving you a hiding, young Master Berkeley?"

"Oh no, Mrs Pinch. She guessed that the vicar was thwacking you, not me."

"Heavens," said Peggy moderately, more to herself. "I mean, good heavens indeed. It seems that Miss Hestey doesn't like Reverend Beamish at all, with her mischievous tittle-tattle about his visits to Larksteer Cottage, now she has him misbehaving with me. She's quite determined to have him removed from our parish. Master Berkeley, chewing on your straw of grass, slouching with your hands in your pockets, you're the picture of a cocky devil who knows what he's saying; tell me, does anyone believe Miss Hestey's nasty wagging tongue?"

"I'm afraid, I've heard some say that treatment for a petulant schoolgirl was no less than you deserved and well done the Reverend."

"Yes, well. Common opinion may be correct. I've learned my lesson, Ernest, let me tell you. Now, come on, what gives our vicar the right to deal so harshly with you."

"Oh, every right, Mrs Pinch. He had the blessing of my folks at home. My old man says that he embarked on fatherhood too late to have the strength for keeping a young man straight and narrow. He has my blessing too, has the vicar because you won't meet a more proper gent. I don't complain. Besides I bargained for it myself on this occasion. I said I'd take a hiding if he kept it all secret."

"So why are you telling me?"

"Because you're a policeman's wife and coppers have to keep their mouths shut, like priests and doctors."

Peggy cocked a doubtful eye; she knew that the youth didn't believe that. No, he was engaging her for a purpose. Well, she would let him carry on.

"In the middle of the night, past one o'clock, he saw me coming out of Polly Gunn's back cottage. He'd caught me before and had made me promise that I wouldn't go there again without I was asked, so I knew that I was in a load of trouble."

"This was the night of the murder?" Peggy asked.

He nodded.

Peggy sat on a wooden crate and brought two sticks of liquorice from her jacket. This was enough to tempt Berkeley's fingers from his pockets at last.

"Ernest, why were you in Polly Gunn's cottage in the middle of the night?"

"Because she is the most beautiful vision beyond this world when she's asleep. I can get into her bedroom without waking her and I sit in the corner of the floor and just look at her. I've been there for hours, sometimes. She's so beautiful, Mrs Pinch, like a proper fairy princess."

"Does she know?"

"She's never opened her eyes so I'd say not. But if she ever woke and told me off, I'd never go there again."

"Ernest, it is important that you stop this – and unless you give me your word, I shall tell Polly what you've been up to."

The lad looked betrayed. He nibbled his lip and stuck his hands back in his pockets. "I've never wished for anything shameful with Polly. I mean, being my age, I wouldn't know how to, would I?"

Peggy told herself to be careful with the innocence of this young mind. "Ernest, this is the most important thing I've ever said to you. What you've been doing is very wrong. Stop it."

They didn't talk for some minutes. Peggy lit a cigarette and stepped out for some fresh air. She saw Alexanader Beamish, a quarter of a mile off, negotiating the cinder path from the vestry. The ground was treacherous in that part of the churchyard. It gave way to a steep slope, full of hoof holes. Half-way down, the vicar stopped and waved and Peggy was about to wave back when she realised that he was calling to Peggy Gunn in the twitchel. It was difficult to see her, because she was hidden by a high hedge, but Peggy glimpsed her pushing an old pram full of cut flowers. Against everything was the sound of Thurrock's steam tractor rattling over the cobbled lane to Home Farm.

So what had the vicar been up to, behind Polly's cottage at one in the morning, Peggy wondered. She stepped to her stack of chopped wood and, moving the axe to one side, perched precariously on the pile.

"Ernest, you've told me these things because you've decided that it's best that I know. So, I'll tell you what I make of it all. You were out and about when Major Corquet was killed. You were probably at Holt's Crossing and came up through Middle Thicket or maybe the woods. Did you call at the hovel in Wretched lane, hoping that Polly would offer an alibi for the early hours of the morning? I don't know. But I don't think that you stayed long. When Reverend Beamish caught you, you were frightened that the Major's murderer might learn that you were near Holt's Crossing, so you persuaded the vicar to deal severely with you but to keep it secret. How lucky that Miss Hestey put me in your place when she walked down her garden path. You've said all this because you're worried that her mistake could put me in danger."

"But you won't let people know that I got the hiding from the Reverend?"

"No."

"You won't tell PC Pinch'em, please."

"No, but surely we can imagine a story less embarrassing to a policeman's wife. I hardly want people to think I've been treated like a naughty girl."

"I'd say it was too late for that, Mrs Pinch. Why, the whole village is talking about your arse."

"Ernest Berkeley! How dare you!" Peg caught his collar with one hand and smacked his cheek with the other.

At once, he was flinching, his head sinking and his shoulders coming round as if to shield him.

She put her hand down; it stung and was already beginning to swell. She wasn't going to slap him a second time. "You are certainly old enough to have learned your manners," she said evenly. "So am I to believe that you're too simple to understand them?"

He was wincing, and rubbing the thumb of one hand into the palm of the other. "You mean calling it your arse? Well, Miss Hestey calls it just the same. She says Reverend Beamish took a leather to your arse and well you deserved it. And when Miss Carstairs said such as you've just said, Miss Hestey declared that you were too much of a Merry Daisy to have your sit-down called anything else. She said that you were something or other ... or other. I didn't understand it, not the words, but she meant that you hadn't given Mr Pinch a baby yet."

Peggy looked away. She hadn't realised that common talk had got so far; she wanted to protest that folk should mind their own business, but she knew that gossip couldn't be gossip if it wasn't nosy. Berkeley's comment meant that everyone blamed Peggy for there being no infants in the Police House. Well, she wouldn't argue.

For a few moments, she watched the breeze stirring heads of dandelions

"So, Master Berkeley, I'm a Merry Daisy, am I?" she said.

"I'm only saying ..."

"I want you to report to me anything that Miss Hestey says from now on. You're my special agent. We need to teach Miss Hestey a lesson."

Ernest perked up. "What lesson, Mrs Pinch? A bucket of potato peelings? I could mix you up something really stinking."

"No, no. I've learned my own lesson, Ernest. I won't do that again. No, I need to be a good deal more ... sneaky."

"Your special agent, am I?"

"Certainly. And to mark the office, you must call me Peggity."

"Then you must pass an important message to PC Pinch'em. Tell him the Black Prince has been kidnapped."

"He sounds like a racehorse," Peggy said. "But I suspect he's a train engine."

Berkeley's eyes widened. "Oh, you cannot call it a train engine, not just a train engine."

"It's something I should know about, Ernest?"

"First, you must understand that everything about the Prince is mysterious. (Polly can't see that, though I've tried with her.) No-one knows who she truly belongs to, or what she's for. It's safe to see her only at a sideways glance or as through a crack in a door. Otherwise, who knows as what spell she'll put on you? That's how it was for me, first time."

Peggy was smiling. "Oh, tell me please."

He said, without taking the limp straw from his teeth, "It was an October night, moonlit with grey clouds moving like as ghosts across the ..."

"Oh, stop it," she laughed. "I don't want to hear a romance."

"But you must, if you're to truly understand the Black Prince."

"Then carry on," she teased. "It was a moonlit night, an October night, with clouds like ghosts. And was there the sound of ravens in the tree tops?"

"If not, there should have been." He slouched against the wooden corner post of the shed. "I was hiding in Farmer Thurrock's barn, past midnight."

"What were you doing there?"

"I was up to something," he replied plainly, but making it clear that he would reveal no more. "I heard someone working in a backstall. I crept down from the loft."

Peggy continued to make a little fun of him. "The shadows cast across your face? The rats stiff in their holes?"

"I peeped through a crack in the hoarding, and there he was. Mr Thurrock building a beautiful ... " He shook his head; he couldn't be satisfied with such a common word but where could he find a better one? "truly beautiful model on a tabletop. Different metals, different strings, different .."

"Exquisite?" Peggy suggested quietly.

"Yes, yes. It was exquisite."

"This was the Black Prince?"

"So the farmer's wife told me later. Every man as has seen it, envy has turned to stone. PC Pinch'em included, I tell you."

"And now, the Prince has gone?"

"Too many people wanted to get their hands on it, so Mr and Mrs Thurrock found a hiding place for it. Except, they didn't know that Boy Berkeley was watching as they locked it away. When I went there, the morning after the murder, my first thought was 'Steward Orton has gone and stolen the Prince.' "

"Why would Mr Orton do that?"

"Now that the Major is dead, Jonesy and him will say that the ownership's in doubt, so I bet Steward Orton stole it on Jonesy's behalf. I went and checked and there it was: the cupboard in the barn, broken open. And the train, gone."

"You want PC Pinch to investigate?"

Berkeley shook his head. "You still don't understand. Mr Pinch'em and Verger Meggastones have sworn an oath to act as honest godparents of the Prince. When the argument started, between the Major and Farmer Thurrock, the guardians promised that it would never fall into the hands of a man without good title."

"Ernest, why all this fuss?"

"Ah, you ask because you haven't caught the romance of it. You do not know as what men will do for it."

She knew that Berkeley was waiting for her to drop the remnant of her cigarette. "Where's Tom Hall?" she asked.

"I don't know, Mrs Pinch."

"Peggity I said."

"I don't know and if I did, I couldn't say. Peggity, Mr Halls didn't kill the Major as neither did I."

"I know that. That's why you've told me. You've worked out that the longer Tom stays hidden, the worse it will be for him. He's told you that he's going to lie low until the murderer is caught. But, you see, Ernest, that won't do. My father was a policeman, did you know that? And my Uncle Bertram, and other policemen were always in our house. Every year, I used to go to the policemen's picnic, then I'd be in the middle of scores of them." Sitting in the vicarage garden, with the goats and the donkey not far off, it was easy to remember those Summer galas. All the policemen were old, because the young ones had gone off to fight. For most of her childhood, Peggy thought that a man had to be old before he could be a policeman; it had seemed a sensible convention. "That's why mother asked me to marry Mr Pinch," she explained. "She was very sick. She was going to die, Ernest, and she thought it was one of the last good things she could say to me. She knew I would make a good wife for a policeman and, one day, I will. I'll make my mother proud of me. I will."

"Too right, Mrs Peg."

"She knew I'd make a good job of it, because I know policemen's ways."

"I know a policeman's ways too, Mrs Pinch. Haven't I had him running in the wrong direction, night after night." He tapped his temple. "You have to get inside their heads, you see."

"Let me tell you, Ernest. If Tom Hall doesn't come to light soon, the policemen will stop asking questions about Major Corquet's killer; they'll be content to look for Tom. Then, when they've got him – and they will, for sure – they'll work hard to hang him, until they've done it. That's their way, Ernest. That's how they'll concentrate."

"Thin Jessie Shipley's house," Berkeley said. "He went off across the heath and that's all I know."

"Off you go, Ernest, and remember everything I have said to you."

Peggy's penance expired at half past ten but she kept working until the lemonade was served. She and Polly Gunn sat in the paddock grass together.

"Oh, you have done well, Mrs Pinch." Then the girl frowned suspiciously. "Boy Berkeley hasn't been cheating for you?"

"Certainly not. You must tell Reverend Beamish that I found it quite exhilarating and I am thinking of coming regularly. It's good for my spirit and good for the parish, will you tell him? That Boy Berkeley puzzles me. Were you watching, Polly? When he thought he was due for another smack because of his foul mouth, he cowered and ducked, and screwed up his eyes. He quite softened my heart. But I do wonder if he might not be a very good actor."

CHAPTER SIX

Thin Jessica Shipley had decided that she would allow no-one inside Larksteer Cottage. For one thing, living downstairs had made the place too untidy. For another, she wouldn't be able to cope with their questions. It had become obvious that she hadn't climbed her stairs for months. Tom said it. The vicar said it. Lady Anne said it. From now on, if anyone turned up, she would keep them in the yard.

Jesse expected to see no-one that day. Tom Hall was in hiding, the vicar would stay clear, and her father hadn't called in weeks. Scrubbing the bins in the cottage yard, she kept half an eye out for Lady Anne but she too had reason to keep away. But when she sat on the stump at the front of her house, with a beaker of home-brewed ginger beer and a dish of braised onions, it was Peggy's figure that she saw wheeling her bicycle over the rough boundary path in the middle of the afternoon.

"Good afternoon, step-mother." The welcome was a joke, 'though neither of them laughed. "I see you've shown up the Grunting Pig for what he is. Can I help next time?"

"No, Jesse. I'm rather ashamed of it all."

"Bilge! More likely you've learned to be more crafty. You can't come in. I've got cupboards out all over the floor and I've been plumbing under the sink. Blood and muck everywhere."

Jessica's face was marked with livid pimples. Her forearms had scabs where she had picked at her skin.

"You're poorly, Jesse," said Peggy. "I can see it in your eyes. They're worn out and sunken." She looked up and noticed the grime on the first floor windowpanes. "And Larksteer needs tending to."

"Is that what Grunting Pig has sent you to say?"

"No-one's sent me, Jesse. I know that Tom Hall was here after the murder. Furthermore, I'm sure that the vicar was with you on the same night."

Jessica carried her beaker and plate into the yard. "I love the birds." She held her arms in the air. "I love the way they swirl around my cottage roof, then soar away and do other things until I am ready for them."

What was she talking about? 'Love the birds?' Peggy had heard her curse them for their noise and mess, and the damage they did to her eaves.

Jessica twirled in a circle. "Oh, and sounds of the foxes at night, and the quickness of the hares, and the charm of the little weasels and stoats. But most of all, I like to come out here at night and talk to little fat creatures who make their homes in the black corners of my yard. I called them 'Smudges'. They're hedgehogs and toads."

"Jesse, please."

"I don't like mice," said Jesse. "and the scavenger's not been round in months. I suppose he's living at the Thurrock's place now. There's more for a mangy mongrel there. Nothing here, but broken mangles and buckled wheels. Where does the oil and grease come from, Peggie? Shouldn't be oil and grease in Jessica's back yard."

"Jesse. Please, listen to me. I was at my garden gate when Major Corquet was shot. Miles away. I knew nothing about it. I stayed there for an hour, looking up and down The Street. I said I was keeping an eye out for dear Miss Carstairs' cat but really I was waiting for Pinch to come in."

"Good God, don't tell me you can't sleep without the Grunting Pig!" Jessica discarded the crockery and put her hands on her head. "Bed must be horrible for you."

"It's a matter of the house being closed for the night."

"Thought so. Thought, 'she can't look forward to suffering him'. Oink, oink!"

"I suppose a grown-up daughter can talk about her father like that," Peggy conceded.

"God, break out of it, Peg! He treats you disgusting and it's time you laid down some rules."

Peggy said nothing. Watching Jessica's carrying-on, she realised that she would never be able to explain her attraction to this man. How could she, when Jesse despised him so rabidly? She remembered an afternoon, three years before they were married, when Pinch saved a young child by raising a wagon axle. Everyone praised his selflessness, for the cart could easily have crushed him during the attempt, but Peggy would have none of that. There wasn't a person in the village who wouldn't put a child's safety above their own. No, Peggy admired the raw strength that Pinch had shown. The muscles that bulged in his neck. The sure grip of his large hands, turned raw by the trial. Piggy didn't see her village policeman simply lifting a farm cart; she saw a man who could lift the world. He was the man who could lift her out of any turmoil, if he wanted to.

The early days had been a crush, she knew that (and Muriel Moorcroft had teased her enough times for it). It had nothing to do with love. But the thrill was re-inforced, time and again, with stories and stolen glances that became more and more powerful. Then, she had found herself sitting at the bottom step of her staircase, listening as her mother sought Pinch's advice about her daughter's future. He didn't suggest that he should play any part in it, but Peggy was overwhelmed by the sensation of this man prompting what was to happen to her. To do what he said would be something like holy penance. She didn't dream of him that night; she stayed awake in her bed and longed for him to master her.

In those days (those silly days) she had no idea that he could be a drunk and a bully, or that he could take pleasure in being hurtful to her. When she found out, it was difficult for her not to think that this was the penance.

Peggy said quietly. "The sinner should be careful, or she will get what she prays for."

"Bilge! That's what Carstairs used to tell us. But I know you've more spirit than that. Do you know what I think about your fun with Horse-hips Thurrock? Right idea, wrong head. Throw the slops over the old man's head, Peg. He deserves it." She said, "You and me could help each other. That's what I was saying to the vicar."

"Jessie, your secrets with the vicar are bound to come out, very soon."

"Oh, have you got the wrong idea, girl!"

"The man from Scotland Yard will work it out quickly enough. He's bound to ask you questions."

"What do you mean?"

"For all that time, when I was at the garden gate, Reverend Beamish didn't walk from the vicarage to Polly Gunn's cottage in Wretched Lane. I would have seen him. Yet, he caught Boy Berkeley coming out of her home at one o'clock. If he had spent the evening, here, at Larksteer Cottage, it would have been convenient for him to come into the village that way. Along the railway line, up through the middle thicket and across Thurrock's Top Field to Wretched Lane." She produced the cigarette lighter. "Pinch found it in Middle Thicket. It came from Larksteer, didn't it?"

"You've got it wrong, Peggy," Jessie repeated. "Alex Beamish was here that evening and, yes, he picked up the cigarette lighter from my mantelpiece. But he didn't come to see me and the lighter's not mine. It belongs to Anne Corquet."

"Lady Corquet?"

"They need somewhere to be alone. Larksteer's the ideal place for them. It's a remote cottage in the parish, so the vicar has excuses to call here, and it's on the boundary of Lady Anne's estate."

"The vicar and Lady Corquet? The Major's wife and our parson? No, Jesse it would be too much of a scandal. Oh, this is awful. How long?"

"They've been muddling ducks for six months or more. You leave them alone, Peggy Pinch. Lady Anne is a good person. That's why I said Tom Hall was to go directly to Manor Farm and tell her everything. Yes, I took him in on the night of the murder, but I sent him off to Manor Farm. That's how much I trust her Ladyship."

"Then I must speak to them both. Right away."

CHAPTER SEVEN

When she reached the courtyard of Manor Farm, Peggy saw a Morris Oxford parked at the elaborate porch. Inspector York was leaning against the car's bodywork as he smoked. The canvas roof was up and the driver, in a policeman's uniform with motorcyclist's gaiters, was wiping the split windscreen. Simultaneously, Tom Hall came striding from the stableyard, Lady Anne appeared on the front steps and Peggy started to tread across the washed shingle; three parties converging on a centre. York stood up straight, squeezed the cigarette dead and tidied the raincoat on his shoulders. Peggy thought, 'I'm too late. He's come to arrest poor Tom,' but the detective was looking at Lady Anne's drawn and sorry face.

"I don't know what to say, Inspector. I'm so desperately lost." The widow pleaded, "There must be some other way."

So far, York had kept his back to Peggy but when she got within a step or two – and she was asking herself if Lady Anne could really have murdered her husband – York turned around: "Come with us, Mrs Pinch. Please don't make a fuss."

Peggy caught her breath. Her hand was at her throat and her eyes turned blankly from one face to another. Already, the uniformed constable was at her shoulder and holding the car door open. He gave her no chance to walk away.

Lady Anne kept coming towards them; she was shaking her head and had tears in her eyes. "I'm so sorry," she repeated quietly and Peggy could feel that the woman wanted to reach forward and embrace her.

"I haven't done anything," Peggy whispered. "Are you arresting me?"

The constable pressed a hand between her shoulders, gently encouraging.

"Please, I haven't done anything."

"It would be better if you came quietly," York advised.

Lady Anne and Tom Hall were standing together now.

Peggy moved no further towards the car. She felt herself getting flustered, and summoned up the anger to counter it. No, she wasn't going to let them take her. Damn it, she was going to fight them.

"I didn't kill him," she said. Then more loudly, "I haven't killed anyone!"

York put himself between Peggy and the spectators. "You are not under arrest," he explained. "We are taking you away for your own safety. If you prefer, I can invent some suspicions that you have harboured a murderer. They wouldn't support a charge but they would be enough to hold you."

"Utter rubbish," she muttered spitefully.

Lady Anne stepped forward. "Come into the house, Inspecor York. There must be another way of doing this. Please, don't take her away."

"Mrs Pinch, I want to be sure that you are safely out of the way. I can't allow you to be tempted to run back home. I think you are in great danger."

"What nonsense." She looked at the different faces. She wanted to show that she was unconcerned about the detective's talk of danger, but everything inside her was in knots. "I thought you were a fair man, Inspector. But I was wrong. Pinch could teach you a thing or two about how to treat people."

He relented. "If Lady Corquet can allow a safe and private place, a private room, somewhere?"

The policemen took her to an old servants' storeroom at the side of the house. The walls had been white-washed and the floor was red tiles. There was a breakfast table with two benches of heavy old oak, but nobody had sat in this room for years. A discarded portrait of Lady Anne's great-grandfather had been propped against a wall for so long that he'd stopped caring about how it felt. Four wooden chairs were stacked in a corner. There was a single bulb hanging from the ceiling on a long twisted cord, frayed and stretched in places. The shade was caked in plaster dust and, because the three intruders had stirred up the old place, more of the same dust soon got into their throats and noses. The constable stood like a sentry at the door, at first. Then York told him to relax and he joined them at the table. All three lit cigarettes.

York commenced, "I have spoken to Tom Hall and Ernest Berkeley. They both say that Major Corquet was shot by a man standing at the lineside huts. Harry Thurrock was seen walking in that direction twenty minutes before the murder. When I questioned him, he said that he'd received a telephone call demanding a meeting."

"You mean the Major called Mr Thurrock to a meeting at Holt's Crossing —- and Harry shot him!"

"The exchange operator remembers putting the call through. She recognised the voice and no, it wasn't Major Corquet. It was PC Pinch."

"You can't think that my husband told Harry Thurrock to murder the Major. Inspector, that's silly."

"For a start, I don't believe Thurrock killed anybody. I don't think he got as far as Holt's Crossing. Mrs Pinch, I do believe that you poured slurry over Mrs Thurrock because you had discovered her affair with your husband."

It wasn't slurry, she wanted to say.

"Do you know that Mrs Thurrock is expecting a child?"

She shook her head. She couldn't explain her feelings but she was determined that Pinch would never be charged with murder, no matter how much she had to lie.

"I need to complete my enquiries," said York. "But if the child is a Pinch child, then, I believe, your husband intends that you should divorce him."

"Nonsense."

"People say that he treats you intentionally badly. People feel sorry for you, Mrs Pinch."

"I won't have it. He never hits me, he allows me money. I am much younger than my husband, Inspector, and sometimes that can be difficult."

"But if you divorced him, he could marry Edna Thurrock and legitimise his child. You've not been able to have a family together, have you?"

"We've not tried."

"There are new laws, Mrs Pinch. A woman has been able to bring a divorce case against her husband for three years now."

"But I never would."

"And a man can legitimise a child through a subsequent marriage."

"But how could anyone marry Edna Thurrock? She already has a husband."

"I believe it was your husband's intention to frame Mr Thurrock for murder and have him hanged."

"Oh, Inspector, this is all ludicrous."

"Which part, Mrs Pinch?"

"And for God's sake, stop calling me Mrs Pinch!"

"Which part is incredible? The affair, the pregnancy, the phone call or his treatment of you?"

She tried to reason. "It could not work in the way that you say. Let's start with your ridiculous idea that Pinch wants to divorce me. Right, what are the Chief Constable's rules about marriage?"

"I don't know," York conceded. "Each Force has its own regulations. I'm an outsider, you know that."

The police driver explained, "A constable over twenty-six years old with more than three years service can ask the Chief's permission. It has more to do with the supply of married quarters than the Chief's view of young weddings"

"And if the young lady is already pregnant?"

"The constable is required to resign."

"There, Inspector. Do you think that the Chief Constable would allow PC Pinch to marry the farmer's widow?"

"Believe me," York said coldly. "When this is over, Mr Pinch won't need to ask anyone's permission to do anything. He will no longer be a policeman, however the case goes."

Peggy had no answer to that. She could only repeat, "I will never divorce my husband. I take my marriage vows very seriously."

"That is why I believe you are in danger, Mrs Pinch. You are now an obstacle to his plans."

"Pinch?" she asked. "Where is he?"

"He's busy," York said. "He's not been arrested but he won't be in the village until ..."

"Until you say so?"

He nodded. "Until I say so. Until, you are safe."

Peg sensed that they were underneath the main house. She heard the groans and arousals of a grand Aga above them, and the sounds of people treading across the gravel outside seemed to be on a higher level than the floor of their storeroom. This would be a damp and cold place to sleep, Peg thought. She noticed that no cushions or fabrics had been left here; nothing that the mice might want to nibble.

"Inspector York, you say that I'm not detained. I'm only here for my own safety. You think that my husband means to hurt me. Well, now that I have been warned, surely it is for me to decide what I need to do. If I'm not detained, I'm free to go. I'd like you to return me to the village."

York stood up. He said, as he walked towards the door, "The constable will be standing outside." Then, on the point of leaving, he asked, "Can you tell me anything about a replica locomotive?"

"The toy train," Peggy sighed. "Inspector York, I cannot."

"Farmer Jones tells me that there was a dispute between the Major and Harold Thurrock; it could have been about a model locomotive."

"What would Mr Jones know about that?"

"He knew that the Major had hidden it for safekeeping, suspecting Thurrock wanted to steal it, but when Jones went to take possession of it, this morning, it had gone missing."

"Then surely, you should ask Mr Jones what he was up to. No, I have never seen the toy, and the only story I've heard says that the Major was likely to steal it from Thurrock, not the other way round."

Left alone, Peggy looked around the white walls and the bare floor and suddenly felt that she was miles from anywhere. It was too soon to be in another cold and colourless room, after her night in the police cell. The cell had brought on an isolation that weighed more heavily on her mind as each quarter hour passed (and this room would be the same). Last night, she had known that she could shout as loud as she liked and no-one would hear. She had been under Pinch's control, absolutely. In the worst hours, she had withdrawn to one corner of the cell, where she made a camp with her blankets and nightclothes. Sleep had been out of the question. But she had known, if she tried hard enough, she could convince herself into a hazy state that was just as deep. She could think herself into another world, below this one, where temperatures and heartbeats, where seeing right and breathing right, weren't important.

In the storeroom, she stood up from the oak table and started to walk about. She began to tell herself the story of the murder night. "At twelve o'clock, I went to my gate and looked for the Queen O'Scots..." but Lady Anne knocked on the door and walked into the room, before Peg's recollection had properly started.

"Oh!"

"My dear, you mustn't worry." She was composed and friendly, and was ready to speak without any sense that she needed to be wary of what she was saying, or that she needed permission to cross boundaries. But Anne Corquet had no loftiness about her. Her rather chubby face, naturally sloping shoulders (for which every nanny must have reprimanded her), and her uneven feet had always held her back from assuming any authority that others didn't press on her.

She smiled at Peggy – and her eyes went down at the edges, as if they might fall off the sides of her cheeks, and her mouth dropped in a way that would have looked sad on any other face. "Dear Peggy," she said, offering her hand. "Oh, you poor dear thing." She didn't suggest that either of them should sit down.

Peggy was saying, "Lady Anne, I'm so sorry. What happened to your husband is something that none of us in the village can be forgiven for. I am sure that you sense the sympathy that people want to express."

"My husband made enemies. This wasn't the first night that he'd walked at night, knowing that someone might want to settle a score. The matter needs to be dealt with. Captain York didn't want me to see you but I was persistent."

"Captain York?"

"Oh yes, the 'Corkers' and the 'Yorkies' have known each other for years. I wasn't surprised when he purloined the murder for himself. Listen, my dear, I can't stand in the way of his proceedings but I want you to tell Pinch that I haven't squealed. His secret is safe."

"I don't know what you mean."

"Oh yes you do. Why else would you toss kennel waste over poor Edna Thurrock?"

"Lady Corquet, I promise you, it wasn't anything so foul as kennel waste."

"Pinch was not the Thurrocks' first choice," Lady Anne disclosed. "They approached the Major but he would have nothing to do with the pair. Hardly a couple you could trust to keep quiet. If the arrangements had ever become public, why, the scandal would have lasted for years. But please, tell Pinch that his secret is safe.

"Now then, the others. Yes, I told Tom Hall that I was summoning the constabulary and if he was going to run off, he'd better get going. But Tom knew that he had nothing to hide; we'd done a lot of talking, Tom and I. Now, Boy Berkeley I'm not so sure about, and I've put Yorkie on his tail. You see, the Major was wary of meeting Thurrock on that evening, so he paid the Berkeley boy half a guinea to scout the area and make sure that he'd come to no harm. I've half a mind to ask for the money back. Not for myself, you understand, but for the Major; he was a stickler where the servants were concerned."

"Why should Ernest Berkeley murder the Major?"

"Lord knows. Probably thought that half a guinea wasn't enough. He'd be after the other half. Don't take me too seriously, my dear. Tom was there and says Berkeley couldn't have done it. Yorkie has agreed that I shall run you back to the village. (You'll just love the tourer at full throttle with his open top. It has a lovely growl.) We don't want everyone to see policemen delivering you to the doorstep, do we? But he insists on placing a policewoman in your house. This is for your protection, Peggy, and you must not object." She reached for Peggy's cold fingers. "Just for a few days, just to be safe. Pinch won't be home before teatime. He's been preparing police headquarters for the emergency. Oh God, girl, not on his own, I mean!" She leaned forward to confide, "But he knows nothing about your detention."

"Then I shall tell him," Peggy declared.

CHAPTER EIGHT

"The truth!" Pinch, red from the neck up, slammed his fists on the kitchen table. He was an angry kettle rattling on the hob. His collar was ready to burst and his ears stuck out with fiery tips. Blues and whites were sharp in his eyes. "I stand humiliation," he shouted. "I expect humiliation. What else does a man bargain for when he takes a wife a generation younger? But I won't be shamed!"

Peggy was plain faced and at a loss. Why was she in the middle of this row when there was so much else to say? She'd had no chance to warn him of the assignment of a WPC, or tell him about her interrogation in the Manor House cellar. Someone was sure to tell him that she had arrived home in Lady Anne's motorcar. If she kept these stories to herself for much longer, she would be deceitful. Later, he could say that she was hiding matters from him. She needed to get them out in the open.

To begin with, she had been working at the sink, and let his tirade of harsh words beat against the back of her head. But his temper was gathering pace and, if she did nothing, he'd boil over. She turned and stood before him with a cloth in her hand. "Pinch, we need to talk," she said for the third or fourth time.

"No!" The fist slammed down. "We will not talk! You will tell me the truth!"

"Please don't be like this. People are saying that you're mean and horrible to me and I'm saying it's not true but now ..." She worked hard to hold back the tears. "You're proving them right."

"I know what people are saying. The talk is all through the village – that my wife bared her arse for the vicar to thrash."

That word again; she hated it.

"You know that I'd never allow another man to do that."

"I can't take it, woman." His anguish showed through the cracks in his voice.

" I'd never show myself off. Oh God, Pinch, think straight."

"Say it."

"I didn't."

"Then say it."

"I didn't do it."

His face was even more intense now. He studied her eyes for any flinch or flutter that he might take as guilt. She had never seen him so angry. She knew that she had to do something. Somehow, she had to give him a way out. She tried to think of things that he would want her to say. 'I love you, Pinch,' 'I'll do what you want,' 'I'll be good.'

But no. She pictured herself as a child desperate to placate a fuming father; it wouldn't do.

She slapped the wet cloth on the table. (It sounded more violent than she intended.) She stood with her feet square to the floor, her hands in fists at her side and leaned forward. "You cannot believe that I would do that!" It came out as a shout. Quickly, before he could shout back, she said, "And don't say 'arse' at me! I hate the word." Her husband was close to violence, but she stood firm.

Then his great fist thundered on the table top. A vase rattled across the wooden surface and toppled to the floor. The sound of splintering glass let loose the hounds of hell. He leapt at her, his voice roaring, his body broader than ever. Peggy fled backwards, crouching in front of her sink.

She covered her ears and screamed. "Don't rape me!"

The words were out before she knew it. She looked up and saw his face, heavy with sweat, bearing down on her. "I'm sorry," she was mumbling. "So sorry. Pinch, I'm so, so sorry."

He took half a step from her, raised his hand, backwards and high up.

"Don't!"

She saw just a flicker of hesitation in his eyes.

"Don't," she said again, her face taut, her voice shrunken. "You have never struck me, Arthur Pinch."

He didn't move.

"Do it, and there's no way back." She said, "Which one do you want to be? Arnold Flowers who beats his wife after the Red Lion have thrown him out, or Truscote who takes his belt to dumb Mildred's hide?"

His red hand relaxed. Slowly, it came down to his side.

She straightened, lifted her face and made no attempt to shield herself. "Nothing happened at the vicarage," she repeated quietly, her throat swollen, a headache digging at her forehead. "You don't believe me, do you?" The tears filled her eyes.

"Show me," he said.

"Oh please don't say that. I can't. You know that I can't."

"Which makes your obliging our vicar all the more sinful."

She wanted to say, make me do this and I'll never forgive you. But what would he care? "I didn't," she pleaded in a voice that was giving in. "I didn't do anything."

He stepped back to the table, took the chair in one hand and threw it aside. "Show me!"

"If you tell me to, you know I will do it. I have never disobeyed you, Pinch."

He waited – and all the little sounds in the kitchen became loud. The clock, the seeping plug, the draught in the larder. He read Peggy's face, every sinew was pleading 'no'. But, this time, Pinch needed to be certain of the truth. He nodded.

"You will go into the parlour," she said very quietly, "while I prepare. You must give me time."

Drained of his bad temper but still feeling foul, Pinch adjourned and sat at the parlour window. The jigsaw of horses and carts was still unfinished on the table; he hadn't touched it since Peggy's night in the cell. The newspaper, the dispatch from the town's police station, and the flimsy parish newsletter lay, unopened, on the windowsill. Pinch slouched, and crossed his legs; he put his chin in his hands. It was hard for him to look grave without looking sulky. He couldn't hear Peggy moving in the kitchen; he'd give her another three minutes.

Outside, the Thursday afternoon bus shook on its wheels, made a sound like a courted duck and pulled away from the War Memorial leaving a fat policewoman in a tweed jacket and a skirt of different sizes. She looked as if she had been deposited. She stood on the grass bank, with a suitcase and a bundle in a blanket, and ran a hand through her unruly hair. She hailed two of the children who were bicycling from the top of the village to the bottom and demanded that they should carry her luggage across the road to the Police House.

"You don't want to go in there," said the youngest. "All hell's been going on. The whole street has been hearing it. Miss Hestey and Miss Carstairs were leaning over her front fence for twenty minutes. That's how long it lasted. Mrs Porter even closed the Post Office early."

"Get on with it," she snarled.

She followed them, barking more instructions and moving in a way that brought sniggers and ridicule from her porters' playmates. Her body was like a pile of children's building bricks threaded together with string. The top half rocked on the hips; it would never fall off because the base was so big but it wobbled on the point of getting cricked. Pinch made little of her approach. He recognised the armband and the ribbon around her hat but he thought, idly, that she must be an auxiliary (surely, she was too hefty to be a sworn-in constable). She was probably delivering a special packet from headquarters.

"We could do with more coal," he muttered to himself. "We don't need more circulatories or orders."

"Leave the bags there," she barked when the children reached the front door. "Run off, you lot. I don't want to see you watching. Go on!" She spent a couple of minutes tucking and straightening before she knocked.

Pinch got to his feet. He crossed the parlour carpet and pushed the kitchen door open. His wife was standing at the sink again, facing the window and the back garden. She was still fully clothed. She hadn't done anything in the last twenty minutes, just stood. She said, without turning her head, "Please, Pinch. I said, give me time."

"Someone is calling on us."

Another rap on the front door pre-empted further talk. He left the kitchen without a word.

"WPC Six," announced the woman at the porch. She was exactly the sort of woman that Pinch couldn't stomach. Flabby-faced, thatch-haired, and forearms like a blacksmith. Her shoulders were too big, and weighted too far forward, so she carried them like a milkmaid's yoke. He knew that she would bully her betters over matters she didn't understand and would swear that going off at half-cock was the best medicine after a late start.

She produced a letter from the inside of her blouse. It bore a crease from her corset strap. "A note here, from the Superintendent at Critchley. He says I'm to help in any way that I can." She closed her eyes when she spoke and twice ran her fingers through her hair. "I'm to stay here until Tuesday next. Call me Six, everyone does."

Pinch couldn't understand her arrival. "The Superintendent sent you from Critchley?" he said, trying to catch up.

"No, no. The Super's from Critchley. I'm from Hayers Martin."

"And you're to stay here?" he frowned, shaking his head. He held the door only half open and tried to block her view.

She nodded, her eyes closed, her hand itching to comb her hair again. "Because of the extra burdens. Because of the murder and the forthcoming emergency." She picked up the suitcase and tried to step inside but Pinch wouldn't move. "I'm to stay here," she repeated. "Until Tuesday next."

"Tuesday next?"

Peggy was at his shoulder. "Captain York did mention it, dear." She was trying to speak like the women on Miss Carstairs' wireless. "I meant to tell you but we've been so busy, haven't we? If it's a surprise, it's my fault."

"We don't need any help," said Pinch, not giving ground. "You can't stay here."

"Yes, well. It's not your house, is it. So it's not your place to say aye or nay." Her eyes blinked, then closed. Pinch waited for them to open again, but they didn't.

"We have the small room at the back, dear," said Peggy.

Pinch turned to his wife, "What's this about?" and the WPC pushed her way in.

"Up here?" she said, dropping the suitcase and the bundle at the bottom of the staircase and commencing a laborious climb. "I'll find it," she called. "Up here, is it, and on the left?"

"In here, Pinch," whispered Peggy, tugging at his sleeve.

"I'm not taking her stuff up, I'm not."

"I'll do it later," said Peggy as she persuaded him into the front room.

"Captain, you said. What's this about? He's not a Captain. Inspector, he said in here."

"He means to sack you, Pinch. We'll lose our living and our home. You won't find another job in the village. We'll have to move. Pinch, I've lived here all my life."

The old village policeman couldn't fathom what was happening to him. He started to look at things on the wall. The pen and ink print of The Master's Garden, cut from Reed's Highways and Byways. The barometer that never worked. The nail in the wall where Duggan's lead had always hung; it was painted over now. Peggy was saying things to him but it was too much, too soon. It sounded as if she were talking from another world. 'Just minutes ago,' he kept thinking, 'I was three thoughts away from giving her a good hiding. Now, it's Captain instead of Inspector, a counterfeit peeler's in our spare room, and she's demanding that we behave like ... what? Victuallers who have watered the ale? It only makes sense if she knows more than I do.' He tried to look directly at her but his eyes kept going from the picture to the barometer, to the nail, to the clock and the calendar. "Lose my post?" he said. "Move house? Who's been telling you these things?"

"Our only chance is to solve the murder before Captain York does."

"There you go again. Captain York? I don't understand any of this."

"You've got to make the arrest, Pinch, and take all the credit. The Chief Constable won't dismiss an officer who has saved his people from a killer."

"Dismiss me? Why ever would the Chief do that?"

"Because York suspects you. That's why he's sent his woman here. He wants her to dig and delve, to come up with something that connects you to Corquet's murder. And if she finds nothing to tie you in, she'll keep looking for other things until York's got a list of errors and failings, enough to dismiss you. Pinch, I'm really worried about our telephone calls book. The vicar said that calls from this house are free. I didn't pick him up on that, but if he's told Hestey and Hestey's told York, and now York has told this policewoman, Pinch, she's bound to check on our little book."

"Our Record of Calls? She's after something as small as that?"

"We've got to keep all our registers and accounts away from her, Pinch, and we've got to make sure that York hasn't got enough time to build a file against us. That's why we've got to catch the murderer quickly, and get that woman out of here."

He shrugged his heavy shoulders. "I'm not a detective, Peg. No detective at all."

"We'll begin with your telephone message to Harry Thurrock."

"Your Captain-Inspector knows about that? Lord, he must know nearly everything."

"And what he doesn't know, he's close to guessing. What's worse, Lady Anne has made up her mind that Edna Thurrock's baby is yours. Pinch, you must deny it. No matter who says it, no matter how strongly they argue, you must swear that it isn't true."

"Peggy, there's something you can't possibly know."

"I don't care. Care? I don't even want to hear it. I just want you to deny that woman's having your baby. Not because it will spare my weeping. Not because I couldn't bear to show my face. Not because just thinking about it grips my stomach. But because it will buy us time. Pinch, they've got us on the run. We got to slow them down."

"The truth will come out, Peggy."

"But not before we've caught Corquet's killer. Come on, what did you say on the phone?"

"Then it all comes unstitched. I don't mean only the secrets and excuses, I mean the allowances that we make – we all make in this village – for one another. Matters that we thought we had buried years ago, will rise up and accuse us. The little bits of goodness – like the way we all look after Miss Hestey and why we've kept that hidden. One by one, each thread will be pulled and, you're right, old Pinch stands to lose most of all. The world is about to cave in."

He looked at the ceiling as bumping noises came through from the back bedroom. "What's she doing up there? Peg, she's moving our furniture around. York's sent her to spy on me. God, no one'd believe it."

"Pinch, the telephone call?"

He picked the picture of The Master's Garden from the wall and took it to his favourite armchair so that he could sit with it on his lap. He looked like a child retreating into his own world. Peggy yearned to tell him that everything would turn out all right, but such comfort would have been wrong.

"It started with Tom Hall's story about Corquet letting a young lad die in the war," he said. "He's told it so many times that no one listens any more, but last week, the Reverend Beamish picked up some talk that seemed to give the tale some substance."

"Talk?"

"At an ecclesiastical conference."

Peggy smiled. Pinch usually found long words difficult but he had the kind of mind that could usually find an alternative before the troublemaker was on his lips. 'Ecclesiastical' must have been practised.

"He confronted Corquet but only to allow him the chance to explain it away. However, the Major reacted as if he had been caught out, good and proper. He immediately offered to buy the vicar's silence. Now you know that Alexander Beamish would have been horrified by any such proposal, but I mentioned that the Thurrocks were struggling to keep their farm afloat. I also hinted that they were thinking of starting a family and some extra funds would be welcome. I said, if the Major wanted people to see what a good fellow he was, he could help the Thurrocks out. That's why I telephoned old Harry, so that he could meet the Major at Holt's Crossing and agree terms of the gift in secret."

"But he never got to Holt's Crossing," Peggy objected.

"Curiosity got the better of him."

"Curiosity?"

"Stupid nosiness, more like it. As he passed Larksteer Cottage, he saw Lady Anne's figure at a window. He crept up and peeped in; he saw the vicar and the lady spooning in Jessie's front room. That's what he told me when I called at his farm, the day after."

Peggy brought her fingers to her nose and stifled a laugh.

"What's so funny?"

"Spooning? I never thought I'd hear you say that."

"Well, please do carry on. Laugh at me in my own house."

"I'm sorry, Pinch."

"He was there when the train went through the valley. All three of them have an alibi, Peg. The vicar, Lady Anne and Harry Thurrock."

"But if the vicar was in Larksteer Cottage, who was in Middle Thicket?"

"I was. I'd gone to observe Thurrock's meeting with the Major. That's why I knew that the cigarette lighter had been dropped near the thicket later in the night or early in the morning."

"Yes, the vicar had picked it up from Jessie's sideboard before he left."

"I must have been in Middle Thicket when Corquet was killed, but I didn't hear a gunshot and I didn't see him fall. I wasn't looking at the railway line. I was watching for Harry Thurrock coming up from his fields. Then I saw the vicar's figure, walking along the path from Jessie's cottage. I didn't see the goings of Tom Hall, but Berkeley ran past me so close that he almost trod on me. I hurried back to the village, all the time I knew the vicar was half a mile behind me. I didn't want him to catch me up. I wanted to be away from the scene without being spotted."

"So you both came back through Wretched Lane."

He nodded.

"Who knows you were in Middle Thicket?"

"York will want to know why I decided that the lighter wasn't there before midnight."

"Don't mention it again," she said. "If he asks, you mustn't tell him the truth. You must fib."

"Peggy, you don't understand these things. When they find out that I've been lying, they'll hold it against me."

"By that time, you and I will have caught the murderer. We're in a mess, Pinch. I can't let us flounder while you try to obey the rules." She thought, 'Leaving things to you saw me nearly ravished and beaten in my own scullery. That's how bad things have got. I have got to stand up, not against you, but for you.'

The hang-dog look on Pinch's face suggested that he was reading her thoughts. He nodded.

"Pinch, you've got to explain to me what you did in the village that night."

"I heard St Stephens chime one o'clock as I crossed the green."

"But you weren't home before twenty past."

"I walked down as far as the memorial when I was caught by Hestey-woman crossing from Back Lane in her night clothes. I asked what she was about and she told me that she had wasted half an hour helping Miss Carstairs' pussy cat from a tangle of junk in Polly Gunn's back garden."

"We don't believe that, do we? On her own?"

"She knocked and shouted, she said, but Polly was pretending to be in a deep sleep."

"Yes," said Peggy. "She does. I'm afraid that Polly and Ernest Berkeley have been behaving foolishly. She allows him to creep into her room and watch her from a corner. Of course, he has promised me that she plays no part in it, but I didn't believe that for one moment. They mean no harm, Pinch, but I've told the boy that it has to stop."

"I had to see Miss Hestey home," Pinch continued. "That's why I was late."

Peggy smiled, "Well, it seems that the whole village was out and about that night, and half of us were looking for Miss Carstairs' cat!"

She allowed herself to think aloud. "No-one saw her. Miss Hestey says she was in Polly Gunn's garden, but nobody saw her there. Looking for Queen O'Scots? I don't know. I think that tempestuous cat can look after herself. I wonder what Miss Hestey was really up to?"

"Peggy," he cautioned. "You've no reason to doubt what she says. Please, don't be too clever. You cannot think that Miss Hestey was firing off shotguns at Holt's Crossing."

"You don't know that she wasn't." But that sounded petulant so she conceded, "I can't think why she would. I have to think how Miss Hestey's life has changed now that the Major is dead."

Pinched asked, "What do we do?"

"You go on patrol. I'll help our WPC settle in. She needs to understand, from the start, that nothing is wrong in this house."

Her husband moved towards the door. His head was low on his shoulders, his hands loose at his sides. "Miss Hestey would like to see me done down," he said morosely. "Corquet's keeper warned me about her. Seems like most people in this village would like to see me nailed for something"

In spite of all that he had done, Peggy still wanted to be there for him, but now wasn't the time to pity him or soothe the man-child within him. Being resolute was the best way she could help.

She knelt at the sideboard cupboard and pretended to re-pack some Sunday napkins. When she was sure that they had no reason to look at each other, she said, "The vicar took his strap to the Boy Berkeley. The Hestey woman heard what was going on but thought I was taking the punishment. She put the story around and Berkeley has been happy to encourage the lie. We'll not dwell on it. Especially the supposed details, if you please."

"There is something in that," he said.

"Please Pinch. Don't make me suffer it all again."

"I can't put my finger on it, but there is something about Hestey hearing what goes on in the vicarage and the Major no longer being around to say she's wrong. I can't make sense of it. I don't understand what's going on." He gave a bear's cough. "Why are we talking like this? Why is that woman upstairs? Why am I the last to hear what my wife's up to? To save my job, you say? Well, I'm not sure."

"Pinch, no." She had the beginnings of tears in her voice. "Please, go now."

Pinch collected his helmet from the rack in the hall and took his coat from the hook. It didn't occur to either of them that she had told him to leave the house, and he was doing as he had been told.

"You won't forget evensong," she said. "You will be back in time, won't you?"

"We'll not go tonight," he said.

"I think we should, Pinch. I really do."

She left him grumbling and went upstairs. Peggy found her guest sitting on the bed, reading from a batch of old letters. She had untied the bundle and opened the suitcase and most of her belongings were on the painted floorboards, but she had placed a cheap photograph in a soft metal frame at the bedside.

"The 'It' girl," she explained, as she stood up. "Clara Bow."

"Oh, I thought it was Bebe Daniels."

"Well, we can't expect a village girl to know the difference, can we? Stuck out here as you are. Poor Clara and I have much in common." She was standing at ease, military style, with her hands on her hips. "Call me Six," she said. "Everyone does. Look, the superintendent has told me all the suspicions about this house, I know what to look for."

"Really, there's no need. Mr Pinch is gruff and easily put out, but he would never hurt me."

"A woman to woman talk later on, do you think?" She put her hand inside her blouse. "Did PC Pinch keep my letter? Damn, did he keep it?"

Then they heard the front gate rattle.

"Ah, gone on patrol, has he?"

Pinch chuntered all the way up the road. He wanted to kick up stones and go 'blast and buggery' but he had a feeling that he was being watched so he chuntered boldly but went no further. The vicar beckoned him from The Red Lion but Pinch wanted nothing to do with the man. Without waving back, he walked doggedly into the dark twitchel that ran between the village lanes. Verger Meggastones, drunk and incapable, would be here before long, slumped against the back fences. Pinch thought about saving his place so that they could damn the world together. But no, tonight he wanted to be grouchy and sour on his own. At the junction with Back Lane, he checked that the coast was clear then crossed over and trudged up the final thread of the soddened footway. He was heading for his favourite hiding-tree at the edge of the village.

His parish beat was worthless, he thought, full of idle and disreputable people. Liars. Like children in a playground, they would spot the weakest character and pick on him. Why say something good, when something cruel is twice as juicy? Devils. He found the old oak, where the twitchel met the boundary of Thurrock's Top Field, and sat down on the blind-side to the houses.

"Bugger evensong," he mumbled. "I won't go."

Pinch thought he had settled for an hour by himself, but it wasn't long before Boy Berkeley scurried along the bank, a satchel of ale bottles over his shoulder.

"I like to hide round this tree, sometimes when Polly shuts herself in and won't let me near." Without invitation, he settled himself at Pinch's side. "She knows I'm not really hiding. I keep poking my head round the trunk until she calls me in."

He pushed a couple of bottles into Pinch's hands. "Here. I sneak them from the vicarage potroom. Old Beamish is not as sharp as he thinks he is. Oh, it's not stealing when it's you, Mr Pinch'em. I've heard the vicar say, a hundred times, 'Pinch, you take one whenever you want.' "

"I suppose it's all right then."

"We can't let it happen, PC Pinch'em. Old Verger Meggastones has got the loco and we both know what that means, don't we? The vicar will be saying that he should have it, and we don't want that to happen, do we?"

"Who says Meggastones has got it?" Pinch asked.

"I heard him bragging to Miss Hestey. He said, after the Major was done in, old Jones dug it out of the hiding place but pretended it was missing. Then Steward Orton said that unless he handed it

101

over, he'd tell the Captain that Jonesy had tried to get his hands on Thurrock's place. So Jonesy gave it to Steward Orton but he bragged to Meggastones who said it was rightly his because Orton owed him money in a game of cards." He swallowed some beer. "Gets complicated, don't it, Pinch'em?

"Then it's Meggastones' fair and square," said Pinch.

"Well, I don't think we should let it happen," Berkeley said. "What's more – Mr Pinchie-Pinch'em – you want to be wary of what my Polly says. Though I tells her not to. She made the noises about the Reverend and your lady. Never a word of it was true. And now she's saying as she saw you coming up the fields from Edna Thurrock's place, the day after the murder. I try to keep her quiet, Pinch'em, but she's a one for herself."

"Never mind all that," said Pinch. "I want you to tell me where you were when the Major was shot."

"Mr Halls'll tell you, sir. I was with him."

Pinch was well down the second bottle.

"The Major was shot, then Tom Hall saw you running up the hill, so frightened that you fell over him. So, how close to the railway line were you? Throwing the gun away was the first thing you did, and I don't think you've been foolish enough to go back for it since. Think on, Berkeley, when they find the gun, they'll hang you for it."

"Not me, sir. I didn't do it, I swear."

"Bloody liar," said Pinch, shaking the beer bottle. "You're like the rest of them. You're all bloody liars."

Berkeley was on his feet and backing away. "I'm not staying round here," he declared. "You've gone mental."

He slipped into the greyness of the farm field. "You're drunk, you are," Pinch heard him shout from far off, but Pinch was busy with his own thoughts and gave no attention to the lad's flight.

Elfrida, his first wife, had told their daughter that Pinch was a grunting pig who was dirty in his trousers, who messed with himself in bed, scratching and wiping all the time. 'I can't live with you any longer,' she had written in her last note. Now, years later – years, and chances later – he feared that he was driving little Peg into the

102

same despair. As the dark thoughts got the better of him, he felt himself growing smaller until, like a gnome or goblin, he became indistinguishable from the moss and bark of the tree trunk and he was ready to disappear into the fairy world beneath the twisted roots.

Now and then, noises from the village brought him back from his reverie. "What goes on here?" someone called, and only the raucous laughter that followed stopped it being urgent. Then he heard some familiar hallowing and barking; Jonesy from Home Farm was turning his wagon in the shallow ford at the bottom of the village street. The church door banged, a sound that carried at any time of day or night. A wife shouted that it wasn't her fault. All these people pretended to know the truth about Constable Pinch, yet Pinch was nowhere near understanding the past ten years of his life. 'Devils and liars,' he wanted to shout. 'You want to see old Pinch done down!'

There's no godliness in here, Pinch, said the gnomes and goblins. You'll find yourself amoungst bent and titchy trolls with organs three times the size they should be, and smells that turn faces green. No singing here, no wailing even, just the croaks and groans of embittered souls. Done-to or done-by makes no difference. Crooked men, all. With crooked sticks to walk their crooked miles. What's the story you're telling, Pinch?

When Pinch looked carefully, he could see the lantern on the corner of his lost daughter's cottage, across the moor. As he studied the scene for any movement, he heard two voices pass behind him.

"Tell me, do you think Tom Hall's a communist?"

"I wouldn't know one if I met one."

The men were walking in Wretched Lane, but the night was so dark and the trees so full that Pinch could hardly see them and he didn't want to show himself.

"He seems to fit the bill." This was York's voice. "He returned here after the war, to foster discontent and turn the common villagers against their local squire. Don't tell me it doesn't happen. I get reports from all over the country. Men like Hall are determined to menace the constitution. There was that Russian letter, a couple of years ago. You know, I don't think the government ever got to the bottom of that."

"Murdering the Major did no-one any good," commented his companion. "He owned no railways or mines, as far as I know."

Risking discovery, Pinch crawled from behind his tree. The stranger was tall with arms too long for his body. Both men wore trench coats and trilby hats.

"Pinch is as good as in the bag, thanks to the Hestey woman. I hope to get a sworn statement from Thurrock in the morning. I'm going there first thing."

"You want me to come along?" asked the stranger. "The woman may seek medical advice."

So York had brought a doctor into the investigation. "A police surgeon from the Met, I'll bet," whispered Pinch. "A dodgy bloody doctor. Now, what's he want one of them for?"

The men had stopped in the middle of the path. Pinch wondered if they had heard him move. They both looked at the high branches of the trees. Then York produced cigarettes from his coat pocket and they went through the rigmarole of lighting them. "The Chief has tabled a visit for Friday. That's when I'll have Police Constable Pinch cashiered. Defalcations and moral ineptitude."

"I feel sorry for all his women," said the doctor.

"I'm hoping to get more from the Thurrocks. I'll be there before breakfast."

Minutes to midnight, Pinch knocked on the schoolma'am's door. "Miss Carstairs, what did my wife tell you on the day she died?"

"Pinch, you dear man. Please come in." Her hair was in its scarf, but she was a long way from being ready for bed. She was wearing carpet slippers and an extra cardigan.

He took off his helmet, dipped his head as he stepped inside, and wiped his feet. "Miss Carstairs, I must speak to you in bold terms."

"No," she said. "Don't say a word until you have made yourself comfortable and I've laid a tray of tea. Hang your coat and hat on the banister post."

Her sittingroom was immaculate. The chairs in this room, and all of the furniture, stood free of the walls, making the place look smaller and wholly focused on the tiled hearth. Miss Carstairs had lived her life alone so there were no photographs but a series of small watercolours were hooked on a pillar by the door. These pictures were survivors from her early days as a teacher. The clock on the wall had been a retirement present. For years, it had been fixed in the entrance hall of the village school and moved to the cottage following a unanimous petition. It was too big for the room. Its round mahoghany case was ten inches deep and sat proud of the wall. The bold black hands and the loud tick-tock seemed to dominate everything – except that Miss Carstairs gave no sign that she noticed it. Pinch decided that it was so ostentatious that it dared not be wrong. He had heard that it had been donated to the village by one of the failing railway companies but he didn't know the truth of that. From the railway station to the village school, to the schoolma'am's cottage.

Close to the fireplace, an upholstered footstool was occupied by several old copies of Woman and Home, the reds and browns of its two tone covers suiting the autumn shades of Miss Carstairs' wallpaper. On quiet evenings, the neighbours could hear Miss Carstairs singing lightly to herself. Pinch thought that was very right for this little home.

"Miss Carstairs, I don't want you to think that any shouting you may have heard from the Police House this afternoon ..."

"I was pleased to hear it." Clemency Carstairs picked some loose fluff from the French knitted tea-cosy, then smoothed it down so that it sat neatly over the round china pot. "Ah, the crisis, I thought. Peggy and Pinch are good enough to come through this."

"It was nothing to do with our marriage. The village is going through a difficult time. People we know well, they don't seem to be quite the people we thought we knew. Sometimes, if you have known people for a long time, you want to cling to your image of them. We were angry about friends, that's all."

Miss Carstairs knew that he had made up the little speech, but she agreed with him. "We are living on shifting sands," she said. "I

105

don't think the world has properly found its feet since the war and the nation is ready to tear itself apart. Here in our village, our close community is learning to doubt the people – the important people – in our little landscape. We are hearing stories about them, every day."

"Miss Carstairs, Elfrida left a note saying that she could no longer be a proper wife to me. I know what lies behind that; it's something I cannot forget, but tell me what she said to you, that day. I know you kept it from the inquest."

"Things might be better left unsaid." Her knitting in progress had been rolled into a ball, skewered with a pair of needles and tucked into the crook of her armchair where it could be picked up at a moment's thought. She pretended to look for it. "Why don't you call me Clemency? We have known each other a long time. Together, we have helped our village in so many ways. Do you remember when I heard that my sweetheart, Benny, had been lost in France? It was you who sat up with me that night, no-one else. You called me Clemency then."

"Elfrida drew away from me in her last two years. She grew to hate me. She told our Jesse that I was something horrible. The grunting pig. But there must have been more. I know that Elfrida was here, in this cottage, during her last afternoon. What did she say?"

The old lady shook her head. "She didn't hate you."

"What did she say, Clemency?"

"She was scared of the Major."

Pinch nodded. He knew that.

"He'd told her that if she didn't finish her friendship with Lady Anne, he would talk to you about it. It was too much for her to face, Pinch. It wasn't your fault."

His face flinched. Had their friendship been so close that it had angered Lady Anne's husband? Pinch knew, of course, that they had enjoyed their special days alone, their treats, they called them. But he had never suspected an intimacy. His razor-savaged face went red.

The old lady was saying, "Verger Meggastones has been to see

106

me. He's worried that the Major's murder will cause people to talk of Steward Orton's old romance with Miss Hestey. It was years ago. A calf love, they'd call it these days."

"But what has Orton got to do with it?"

"Nothing, if things stay as they are, but if Jones takes over Harold Thurrock's farm, there might be advancement in it for the steward."

"I don't understand."

"Well, Jones holds the mortgage, of course."

Pinch was lost. "I still don't understand. Why should Meggastones worry about it."

"Because Miss Hestey is his sister-in-law. Why? Didn't you know?"

Miss Carstairs gave him a few seconds to absorb her comments, then pushed forward. " Now, you must think of Peggy's mother," she said. "Oh, she died six years ago." She nodded surely. "But she does know that you love Peggy dearly. She understands that a husband might not want to press, at first, but I'm sure she is a little disappointed." She poured the milk, then brought each cup and saucer to the pot. She made it look like a carefully planned, well judged manoeuvre.

"Peggy and I, having no children yet?" Pinch ventured.

"It's all right for us to talk, don't you think?" she asked. "You promised to look after Peggy."

"I was there when her mother died," Pinch agreed. "She asked me to marry Peggy and look after her. It was the last thing she prayed for."

"Yes, I know."

"Of course, I had no thought of marrying the child before then."

"But, you see, Pinch, she wasn't a child at all. Peggy was twenty-four when she was left alone in the world, quite a grown up woman. You weren't marrying a bright young thing."

"Twenty-seven at our wedding," Pinch agreed thoughtfully.

"Quite. Many women of that age would worry that they were maidens left on the shelf."

The phrase snagged in Pinch's mind. Could Peggy see herself like that?

"It is all right for us to talk," Miss Carstairs repeated. "You promised to take care of Peggy and I'm like a godparent, living across the road. Her mother is pleased with that, don't you think, with us talking?"

"You are right in thinking that our marriage has not been completed. Peggy is very shy."

"Ah," she said with understanding. It was, of course, a revelation that she had expected and she managed to make little of it. She dipped her head to one side and nodded; a wise old lady, she was indicating, expects to hear of such hiccoughs. "And you'd be reluctant to press her."

"Because I've always thought that she was so young. But, 'a maiden left on the shelf'? No, I can't allow my Peggy to think that."

"She keeps herself to herself, I dare say."

He looked down at Miss Carstairs's neat hands in her lap. "All the time. She prepares for the night downstairs. To keep warm, of course."

"Undresses, you mean."

Pinched nodded. "She undresses in the kitchen and won't come up until I'm in bed. I've never seen Peggy ... as a husband might. Not that I've said that I wanted things otherwise. And, dear me, no, I wouldn't want ..."

"Mr Pinch, of course you would. Of course, you would want. Yes, she always has been shy, even as a child, and more so when she started to grow up. Before you married her, perhaps you only knew the spirited Peggy, stubborn and headstrong. But I remember the young girl I taught at school. If another child spoke about Peggy's appearance, she felt it keenly. I remember one afternoon when the school nurse attended and the children were lined up in their underwear. Peggy was the child who would not look at herself in the mirror."

"A maiden left on the shelf? You don't believe she sees herself in that light, do you?"

"If I might suggest ..."

"Yes. Yes, please, Miss Carstairs."

"Of course, you must let her be shy. She is allowed her own

privacy, aren't we all? But encourage her to prepare for bed upstairs while you undress in the kitchen. So, she will have the bed and you will be coming to her."

"You think so?"

"Yes, I think it might help and, of course, you must emphasise it's because you want to scrub up well before joining her." She said boldly, "You must not be coarse, Pinch. You must truly behave as if Peggy has welcomed you to her bed, as if you are coming to her."

As they stood in the hall, and Pinch was fitting his helmet to his head while Miss Carstairs stood like a lady who wanted to fuss, he asked. "Elfrida's friendship with Lady Anne? There was some impropriety? Enough to cause the Major's anger?"

"Oh yes, Pinch. The Major found Elfrida in his wife's bed."

CHAPTER NINE

"I can't be doing with her," Pinch complained as he chewed the last slice of soggy fried bread and reached for the beaker of beer that would wash it down. He had been indoors for twenty minutes and the woman had been thudding and thumping for all of that time, from room to room, upstairs and downstairs – and now she had turned the Hestey woman away at the front door. "You will have to speak to her."

"She's only trying," Peggy said sympathetically but there was little in her voice to convince either of them. And when she said, "She doesn't understand," her irritation showed through.

"Your Captain York is going to Thurrocks this morning. It will mean trouble."

Peggy thought, 'He isn't my Captain York', but this wasn't a moment to challenge him.

"He's brought a doctor in and he wants Edna Thurrock to swear a statement this morning," said Pinch. "I heard them plotting against me in Wretched Lane, around midnight."

"York and that woman were in Wretched Lane at midnight?"

"No. York and the doctor."

"You must say no, Pinch. Whatever she says, you must say that it didn't happen. When all's said and done, they'll believe a man above a woman. Hestey and Porter will vouch that she's a dizzy who wouldn't remember when her husband shared her bed and when he didn't."

"Don't be clever, Peggy."

"Three days is all I need. I want to speak again with Ernest

Berkeley. Or perhaps not. Perhaps his girlfriend. What's today?"

"Thursday."

"Then I'll know the truth by Saturday."

"That's too late. You're right. York means to sack me, and the Chief Constable's coming to do it on Friday."

She waited and when he looked at her, she said, "Tomorrow, then. I won't let you down."

A thud shook the house, and the policewoman squawked at the top of the staircase.

Peggy looked up at the ceiling. "She's hurt herself."

"Good."

"Oh, Pinchie," she laughed, and said without thinking, "That's naughty." She looked for his reaction.

"You can tell her to stop calling herself a constable," he said. "She's only an ancillary. Not one of these women have taken the attestation."

"You didn't come up, last night," said Peg.

"I was late in. I thought it would be unfair to wake you. I had things to think about."

"Twenty-to-two."

"I was talking to Clemency Carstairs."

"I know, Pinch. I saw you from our window. I wanted to wait for you downstairs but didn't want you to think that I was clockwatching." I put the picture back on the wall for you, she wanted to say. "When I saw you crossing the road, I got back into bed. I thought we could talk but you didn't come up."

He went on chewing.

"I like it when you forget yourself," she offered hesitantly.

Between munches: "Don't call me Pinchie."

She tried further. "We will talk about yesterday, won't we? Not now, but say we will soon."

She saw that he wanted to answer but, before he could finish his mouthful, the policewoman appeared at the kitchen door. Pinch kept his head down. He wanted to move to the back step, out of her way, but her voice started to bellow before he could decamp. "I have told that Mistress Hestey to come back at seven-thirty hours. I

111

said, I'll be on hand today at the Police House so that PC Pinch is free for urgent preparations. I said she's to come back at a proper time."

Pinch got to his feet, pushing the table forward. His face was red, his mouth was full and he gripped his beaker firmly. He snorted impatiently.

"You'll be outside, dear, if we want you," Peggy said with pretended cheeriness. "Strolling up and down the garden path? It's going to be a sunny day."

Pinch grunted and left the women alone.

Peggy looked at the mess of wiry hair and the drawn face and thought, this woman has no idea how to get up in the mornings.

"It's the same in the stations," said the policewoman, breathing deeply to quell any hint of tears. She had woken uncomfortably, with a dry throat and an aching neck. Before she got out of bed, she had heard Pinch grumbling about her. Now, she badly wanted to deliver a job well done. "I never know what I'm doing wrong. Matron says that we'll never be accepted until we take on the commonplace, but when I do, oh, it seems to upset things."

Peggy was about to offer her Pinch's vacant chair but realised in time that the woman was too broad to fit. She passed a tea-cloth and they stood together at the great sink.

"Constable women are new?" Peggy enquired as she poured dripping into a white pot.

"They've got them in London," Six replied.

"But not here?"

She shook her head. "We're allowed. I mean, the Chief Constable could have us properly if he wanted. He invited opinions from all superintendents last year – and all superintendents asked all inspectors – and they said, to a one, that women constables weren't required."

"They would," said Peggy. Through the window, she watched Pinch draw a finger trail of ale on three inches of stone path, hoping that a thrush or his favourite wagtail would be encouraged to come forward and peck. "They're men," she said.

"Even so, the Chief employed the women, called Four, Five and Six, to assist when Matron Gertrude advises."

"What happened to One, Two and Three?"

"He said First, Second and Third Auxiliary would sound too important, so he started at Four."

"There are times," reflected Peggy as she washed Pinch's plate, "when men make you weep with a broken heart and there are times when they just make you weep."

"Oh, there's so much I've got wrong here. Should I go?"

"Not at all, dear. Everything's fine."

Peggy returned some cups to the Welsh dresser.

"It's lovely," said Six

"Miss Carstairs saved it for me from the street auction following my mother's death. Yes, I'm very fond of it."

"I shouldn't have sent the old woman away, should I?" the big woman said.

"Everyone knows that Hestey comes to the Police House for breakfast with Pinch. She's been doing it for two years."

"But Pinch, I thought, took breakfast with the men in the keeper's lodge."

"His first breakfast, yes." Peggy explained, "He comes back for his second breakfast with Miss Hestey but he only pretends to eat. You see, she's not so clever at looking after herself and, left on her own, forgets to take her meals. So she sits at our table and, all the time that Pinch is with her, she nibbles her way through a hot breakfast."

"I still don't see."

"She's made herself poorly in the past so everybody in the village agreed that she should come here every morning. Pinch makes sure that she eats."

"She must be a much loved lady, this Miss Hestey," Six remarked.

"Lord knows, no," said Peggy. "She's a vicious old gossip who would sooner start trouble than say her prayers."

"Then, why?"

"Because if we didn't help, who would? And what would that say about our village?"

"Well, I think it's still very generous of you both."

"Not really. The vicar's morning maid sees that I get four rashers

113

a week and the gardens committee gives me half a dozen eggs. If I spend any extra, it's more than made up for by Pinch's breakfast at the keeper's lodge."

"Oh, I see I've made rather a mess of things. Well, never mind. I'm going to do lost property. I know I'm good at that. Today, I shall see that every item in the cupboard is claimed. I shall take the parcels from house to house if necessary."

"Usually," said Peggy, slowly and carefully though her patience was weakening. "We make sure that either the school or the church women's circle claim the unwanted property."

"Surely not. Surely ..."

"Surely, it is better than the property going to the auction in town? Yes, it is."

"But that's against the rules."

Peggy sighed, "Miss ..."

"Just Six. Please, six."

"I would be wary of calling us a parish of cheats."

"Oh, no. I didn't mean that. It's just that the rules say ..."

"The rules say ..." Pinch had finished his beer and Peggy could hear him trying to bury himself in the bicycle shed. Anything rather than coming back to the house. " ... The rules say that when the wind blows, the bus doesn't come."

With this, Number Six saw something else she could sort out. "It doesn't come? Well, you must ..."

"Our village sits on a hillside and the road from town is unprotected by trees for much of its way, so when the wind is too strong, the bus can't run."

Six nodded. She understood the reasoning, at least, but had no idea what it had to do with her.

Peggy continued. "And anyway, we expect to be completely cut off for two or three days each year. If it's not snow or floods, it'll be a tree fallen down or the road fallen in. There's not a house in the village that trusts the gas or electric and we are all very grateful that Mr Thurrock and Mr Jones keep the wells stout and stable."

"You look after yourselves," said the policewoman, thinking aloud.

"Stand at our gate at eight at night and you'll believe that our village is the only place left in the world."

Six laid the teacloth aside and stood at the open back door. "I'd hoped to catch him before he wandered off."

"We'll not see Pinch before teatime," Peggy remarked. "He'll be about the village doing one thing or another. If you meet him later, tell him I've gone up to Larksteer. They're tidying his daughter's cottage, today."

Peggy made her morning walk through the village last longer than usual. She wanted to be out of the policewoman's way. The Willowby children were of school age but their mother was sick. The ten year old had to look after her and the eight year old wouldn't go anywhere alone.

"Understandable," said Dolly Hoskins, who was waiting for her second bus trip of the week. "Very understandable, and good children too."

When the bus pulled in, Driver David brought news of a false alarm. Yesterday, rumour had it that a coal strike had been called, but the latest word was that nothing would be decided for another forty-eight hours. Peggy paid little attention; news that came by word of mouth was never reliable. (That was the fun of gossip.) This time, she would wait for the newspaper. Dolly couldn't believe that anyone would want to cause trouble on such a sunny day. "Praise the Lord, what a lovely day to be alive."

Jones from Home Farm found the dead dog at first light. He was walking towards Larksteer and stopped to draw from his flask of home-mixed grog at the line of trees, fifty yards from the Idling Pool. He took his time. It was a pleasant morning and Jonesy enjoyed his moments away from the farm. He spotted the carcass early on, but didn't drag it from the pool until he was ready. He recognised her as the vagrant who scavenged between Larksteer Cottage and Manor Farm. He couldn't tell why the dog had gone into the water, but she had trapped her head beneath an outcrop of stone; that was why she didn't come out. He spent twenty minutes burying her. When the people at Larksteer asked why he was late, he told the story with relish; Mr Jones didn't like strays.

Tom Hall, Edna Thurrock and Jonesy were clearing the top floor of Larksteer Cottage. Edna had learned that 'Thin Jessie' hadn't been upstairs for three years (as long as the Pinch couple had lived in the Police House) and, although Jessie insisted that no harm had come to the place, her neighbours decided that it was time to do something. Edna said that Harry would be late, but he was definitely coming. The first task was to keep Jessie out of the way; a tale was drummed up – poor Polly Gunn was deep in a mood of despair and needed a picnic. "We're two of a kind," Jessie had said. "I'll take her up to Ben's Drift for the day. Edna, you will let me have some of your kidney puddings in pots, won't you?"

The three country folk spent the morning emptying the bedroom, all but a few delicate pieces being lifted through the window. They had expected to load two carts with rubbish but so much of it needed to be burned on the spot that there was hardly a need to bring up the horse. (Miles away, Jessie saw the smoke and knew what was going on but she pretended not to realise the truth. Just once, she said, "They'll have found my Nanna's laundry basket. If they don't look carefully, they'll throw it on the fire," but she wasn't distressed.)

At every opportunity, Edna Thurrock looked across the moor. "I want to know where my Harry is. He's been talking in secret with that London Captain and he's too easily led, my Harry is."

Scrubbing began after a cold lunch, with brushes, bristle rollers and a curious water-machine that Thurrock's grandfather had invented to bring mud from the crevices of hard slabs.

Tom insisted that no more than a bare bedstead and a wooden chair should be left in each room. "She'll not climb the stairs. She's as scared as a kitten and if we leave linen or wool up here, things will be back in a mess before Christmas."

"I had a cousin with Jessie's trouble," Edna remarked. "We did it by putting ladders at the windows and letting her see that nothing was wrong inside. Still, it took us a spring and half a summer to get her over it."

The house-clearing carried on, through the chill of a late afternoon. The painting room was the most difficult. Here, Jessica had stored all the pictures she had created during the intense months following her mother's death. Tom worked out that, at her busiest, Jesse must have completed three paintings each day. He kept the others out of the room. He made the papers into bails, wrapped in blankets, which he lowered from the window to the yard. His most important find was a pocket journal, protected in oilskin, hidden beneath the cold ashes in the grate. There had been no attempt to burn it. One look told him that it was the record of a young girl's espionage, her observations of her mother's affair with another woman. He was sure it was something that Jessie would find painful to read. Yet, the diary was too important to leave lying around and too important to throw away. Tom pocketed it. If she asked, he would tell her that he was safeguarding it. However, from the first moment, he had decided that it should pass into Peggy Pinch's hands. She shared so much of Jessica's experiences, old and new, and Tom trusted the woman to be careful of what became of the secret journal.

Peggy didn't join the Larksteer party. Before lunchtime, she heard about the picnic and she tramped across three miles of fields and woods to reach Ben's Drift. There she lazed with Jessie and Polly for the rest of the afternoon. The vicar had recently given Polly a cheap camera and she laughed herself silly, snapping her new friends in funny poses. Peg was sure that most of the pictures wouldn't come out. At five, Jessie set off for Larksteer while Peggy and Polly started to walk back to the village.

"Let's go up to Holt's Ridge and down by the Idling Pool," pleaded Polly.

She was a spritely girl with no figure or grace. Peg didn't know how old she was but this didn't matter; Polly Gunn would always look seventeen and people would always treat her that way. She and her mother had been brought to the parish by Lady Anne's brother and they both worked at the old hall for a time. Then there was a great to-do and the women of the village said that Polly should stay in the cottage and earn her living mending clothes. There was more

117

trouble and the vicar took her on as his morning maid. Her home was a hovel, like all the broken down cottages in Wretched Lane. They had no amenities and no hope of repair. Everyone knew that they would be pulled down, in years to come, and the church would make some money by selling the land. There were other charity dwellings in the neighbourhood so the village didn't need Wretched Lane. But Polly never thought her circumstances miserable. She relished life. She skipped instead of walked, enjoyed falling down and never followed a road if she could cross a field.

When Peggy and Polly reached a stile, on the edge of Thurrock's Top Field, Peggy pretended that she needed a rest. The girl perched herself on a fence post and ran her fingertips through her hair. "What's the truth about Miss Hestey?" she asked.

"She's got a wicked tongue, that's the truth, but when we grumble about her we need to remember that sometimes she's not in her right mind. Some days, she doesn't know who's who."

"That's what I want to know about," said Polly. "I want you to tell me."

This was how village history was handed down. One woman, sitting on a country hillside miles from any house or lane, told a younger woman about matters that needed to be kept quiet.

"She was Steward Orton's sweetheart, wasn't she?" Polly asked.

"That was many years ago. He jilted her and Miss Hestey was taken up by Mr Orton's young bother. They called him Brown's Orton because he worked for Austin Brown, the roadmender. But then, Brown's Orton was sent to France. They promised each other that they would be married as soon as the Great War was over. When she heard that Browns had telephoned the Red Lion, saying that he was at Waterloo Station and on his way home, Hestey waited for him in The Street. She waited all night. Two days later, even when she'd been told that he had been killed on the railway, she still wouldn't be moved from The Street. 'I'm waiting for Orton,' was all she would say. Have you heard her say it? She does, still, when she's mixed up. Steward Orton tried to comfort her and that's when Miss Hestey got confused. Sometimes, she thinks Steward is Brown. Sometimes she forgets that Brown ever existed and that she and Steward are still sweethearts. But Steward Orton had already taken up his position at Home Farm, had married Jasmine Moorcroft's aunt and had his own life."

"That's why people think that Miss Hestey started the fire that killed Mrs Orton," Polly understood.

"If they think that, they're wrong to say it. No-one knows how that fire started, and no-one should blame Miss Hestey, because she may well be innocent of it."

When Peggy didn't answer, Polly persisted, "The Major always said that PC Pinchie knows the truth. I heard him telling the vicar as much and Ernest has told me the same."

"Well, Mr Pinch doesn't know, and he's never said he does."

But Polly was watching her closely. "You don't know nothing about what Mr Pinch thinks. You're pretending because you're his wife and you think you should know."

A two-coach train was travelling along the bed of the valley, its white smoke oddly out of synch with the puffing sounds of the little engine.

"Do you know what the vicar said to Verger Meggastones when they heard that the house-clearing was going ahead? He said they'll find the Black Prince up there. I was listening behind the larder door and, I thought, oh no, they won't because I know where it is."

"It seems to me Polly, that you know so much about what has been going on in our village."

"That's what a vicar's maid is for, isn't it? That's what Miss Hestey always says when she asks me to tell tales. She says, I've come to you, Polly, because the vicarage maid is in the best position."

Peggy cautioned, "It's a mistake for a young woman to think she knows more than she does."

"Do you think they'll find the missing steam train in Jessica's upstairs? My Ernest says there's no place more likely." She sighed, "Most likely, you'll say you know nothing about it."

"Polly, have you ever seen Ernest as nature intended?"

"Without his clothes," the girl crowed. "What a question!" Then she went quiet and nodded. "Not every time but half a dozen times, I have."

"Was he showing that he was ready for you?"

She went on nodding.

"Well, if you accepted him, when he was showing ready, you could have children."

Polly stared hard, concentrating, and the nodding turned to a wagging of her head. "You can't have children until you're married. That's what marrying's for. You marry in front of God so that he knows it's all right to bless you with children."

"No, Polly. If you behave sinfully with a man – whether married or not – you could have children."

"But a baby is a gift from God and he allows it to you after you're married. It doesn't make sense otherwise."

"Do you remember Mollie Green? She accepted her boyfriend in bed."

"She was a very accepting girl, Mollie was."

"And she had a little girl without being married."

"Yes." That was true. But still, Polly wrestled to understand. "Perhaps that was punishment. But no, God wouldn't let a baby be a punishment. Perhaps I shall talk with the vicar."

"No, Polly. Talk to a woman."

"Can't talk to mother," she said with a touch of sulk. "She runs away from me, most times I speak. Finds things to do." She looked up, "I'll talk to you, Peggy."

"Yes, I will always listen to you, but you must stop being sinful with Ernest or you could have a baby."

Still, she doubted. "Even though we're not married?"

"Even though."

Polly thought, then said, "It makes more sense my way." She jumped down from the fence. She wanted to be off and away, but when she saw that Peggy wasn't ready to move, she sat down, cross-legged, in the rough grass.

"Did you accept Ernest on the night of the murder?" Peggy asked.

"Oh, did I! He was strong that night, like a lion."

"Yes, yes, Pol. But we don't talk in too many colours." Peggy reach for the girl's little hand." A lady draws only in pencil, remember. Now then, did Miss Hestey call you?"

That puzzled the girl. "No."

"She didn't shout that a cat was trapped in your garden?"

"In the middle of the night? What would Hestey-woman be doing round our back in the middle of the night? She tells lies. She's a real liar, that one. And I don't believe a word of what she's saying about you in the vicar's library. But don't you worry about her, Peggy; no one listens to that woman. Do you think my Ernie was scandalous with Mrs Thurrock? The Major was always saying so."

"Well, he's no longer here to say his wicked things, Polly, so don't worry."

"No. Thanks to the man that killed him, whoever he is. Anyways," she said, digging two fingers into the ground. "Mrs Peggy, you've got no business talking about me and my Ernie. You want to mind business closer to home. Has Mr Pinch told you that he called Mr Thurrock on the night Corkers was done? Well, it's not true. I heard him at the telephone in the Red Lion, and he was talking to that Edna, not Harold. He's a liar, your Pinch."

Before Peggy could respond, the girl was on her feet and running away. Peg didn't chase her. She let her run on while she walked up the hill at her own pace. The girl stopped at the Idling Pool and stood in an absent-minded way, as if she were thinking up stories or wondering how a sweet or cake might taste. But, as Peggy approached, she realised that Polly was staring at something in the water. She had her fingers in her mouth; her chin was down.

Peggy saw the clothing first. It was bloated because it had been weighed down and air was trying to seep through the top. Then she made out the shape of hips and trouser legs, but they weren't laying right for anybody to be inside, she thought. She saw the chilled white ankles only when she was a few paces from the edge. The ankles were all that had floated to the surface. The rest of the body, face down, was lost in the weeds and dark depth.

They brought up the horse and cart from Larksteer Cottage and took the body away. York stood on the edge of the pond, listening to the advice of the police surgeon. Tom Hall – who had been the

121

one who wrapped Harry's body in blankets, tied at both ends, and loaded him onto the wagon – was washing his hands and forearms in the mucky water.

Peggy and Pinch stood back from the scene.

"Is there any doubt?" she asked.

Pinch shook his head. "Harry drowned himself. He left a note in his jacket for Edna. I found it by the trees. But I want to know what he said to your Captain York, first thing this morning. There's more trouble to come, Peggy."

"Do you want me to go? Shouldn't you be standing with Mr York and the doctor?"

Pinch shrugged his shoulders and stuck out his lip. "I'm leaving them to it. There's nothing for me to do here. Just goes to show. If York was a superior officer in the Force, he would chew my ear off for even thinking of leaving. Here, he'll let me slope off and be pleased to see it."

As they turned away, she linked her arm with his.

"Peg dear, here's hardly the place."

"Show people that nothing's wrong between us, Pinch. I want everyone to see that no matter what's said and done, PC Pinch and his wife stand together."

They walked quietly from the field.

"There's something I can't tell you , Peggy. And if I did, what would you do about it?"

"We need to talk to each other," she said again.

"The joke is, if I could speak up, it might begin to solve so many problems."

Edna Thurrock watched it all from the bottom of the field. The cogitating of people who understood nothing about her and her husband. The doctor and the Lady of the Manor, the owner of Home Farm and the country copper and his wife. There was the detective who wanted to consider the drowning from every angle and distance, kneeling down, stretching over – at one stage, turning his back and looking across his shoulder. As if Harry's death was an incident of science to be weighed before it could be explained. She had told Jones and Lady Anne that she needed no comfort at the moment. Edna knew enough about farms and families to understand that moments needed to be set aside carefully for grief. They were moments that needed their own place.

"No-one will trust a woman who loses her husband in this way," she said to herself. "And Jones will want to talk about money before tomorrow is done with." She was alone, carrying another man's child and, until Jones spoke up, she had the responsibility of running a farm on her own. God knows how she would manage that.

After supper, Edna Thurrock brought Harry's portable gramophone to the veranda and played his favourite music. It was Harry's kind of evening, warm enough to sit outside but with some movement in the air, and a clear sky that allowed the sounds of the valley to carry through the night. 'We'll bring some ale and bacon out later,' he would have said. 'Careful Ed, don't wind her up too much' and he'd want her to use at least three needles during the evening. He loved military records. No concert music for him, and certainly no jazz. She imagined him announcing each piece, not from the label but by identifying the first few bars. Then he would name each instrument playing particular parts, even though he knew Edna wasn't really interested. Edna laughed; gosh, those afternoons when he took time off and played music to his animals instead of working with them. But, Harry hadn't enjoyed that pleasure for two years.

Ask me why he died, she thought, and I'll say the lies did it, intrigues and deceptions that became so entwined that they bound him hand and foot and, in the end, strangled him.

She wanted to say out loud: Harry Thurrock had been a good and simple man who built model railway trains and listened to marching bands. He took risks to bless his wife with a child, but could there be very much wrong with that?

He was gone now.

"Nothing but the truth would stop people thinking bad of him," she said.

Edna walked to the steps of the veranda and, as she listened to the Band of the Aldershot Tattoo, she promised, "The truth will come out. Really, there's no other way. If the tangle of deceit has led to your death, unpicking the mess, one thread at a time, will comfort your soul, Harry."

PART THREE

CHAPTER TEN

The next morning, Polly Gunn, on duty in one of the vicar's greenhouses, saw Edna Thurrock emerge from the churchyard elms and commence her progress down the village street. "She means to call at the Pinch house, Ernie. Do you think there'll be trouble?"

Boy Berkeley, who was eating a generous slice of Polly's seed cake, was confident. "No more than as to scare a sparrow," he said. "Miss Carstairs will be on watch. She won't allow an upset." The postmistress thought so too, but she came to her shopfront to check that the schoolma'am was seated at her parlour window.

Edna Thurrock was marching; she didn't at all look like a widow-woman. She had puddings wrapped with muslin, in a wicker basket looped over one arm. The other hand went backwards and forwards as she strode down the middle of the lane. Perhaps her footsteps were louder than they needed to be. Certainly, she was giving every one a chance to stop and peer. She was a woman of strong words that morning, and she looked straight ahead so that on-lookers had no hope of catching her eye.

Miss Hestey, cross that she hadn't been in the right place to stall the woman with catty questions, flustered: "Pinch needs to know. Pinch in the mix, he must be." And she started out from her front gate determined to track the policeman down.

But Pinch had watched it all from the church kissing-gate, and he resolved to go no closer. Although his own rule usually allowed no smoking on patrol, he took the accoutrements from his tunic pockets and packed a bowl of rich Three Nuns Empire tobacco. "The trouble is of my own making," he told the excited Miss

Hestey. "My lot is to stand and take whatever comes." Thinking aloud, he added, "My Peggy has a good head on her shoulders."

Clemency Carstairs said the same to Queen O'Scots. She let the cat sleep-on in the crook of her arm and postponed taking up her morning's knitting for another hour.

Edna Thurrock knocked rat-a-tat-tat on the Police House door. She stood steady with the basket held before her. (A humorist might have said that she was practising for the shape of things to come.)

"I want to see Peggy Pinch."

"Well, you can't," said WPC Six, who held the door ajar no wider than Pinch had done when she had arrived on the same step, two days ago.

"Of course Edna can," said Peggy at the foot of the stairs. She was surprised that the woman's name hadn't stuck in her throat. "Oh, and you've brought some of your nice puddings, I see. Do come in." She put a hand on the policewoman's shoulder. "Six, the property cupboard, do you think, or the bicycle shed? Mr Pinch won't need you before lunchtime."

"I shall go into the kitchen," Six declared.

"No, Edna and myself will be there. She might want to say things that can't properly be said in another woman's front room."

Disgruntled, broad shouldered Six barged her way out to the front garden (knowing that she could creep around the back and listen).

Peggy offered her hand. "Please come through, Edna." She was managing to make her use of the name sound especially insincere. It wasn't sarcasm, but it was delivered with a cutting edge.

Edna followed the policeman's wife through the house, thinking 'farmers always have too much in their homes'. In the kitchen, she said, "Things need to be settled, Peggy Pinch. No, no, please don't heat up the kettle. I'll say my piece and you might not want me to stay."

"Nonsense." Peggy placed the kettle on the stove. So far, she was very pleased with her own composure. "Pinch says there's no promise of more coal during the emergency. Are you low at the farm?"

128

"Always logs," Edna said and put the wicker basket on the oak table. "Jones from Home Farm has been to see me. 'Quick off the mark, aren't you?' I said. But he's right. The seasons don't wait for mourning."

Peggy thought, 'My God, her husband's not buried yet.'

"Yesterday Captain York questioned me about my condition. He got short shrift, but I knew he'd be back. He's a dog with a bone, that one. I could tell that he's serious about convincing the Chief Constable to sack Pinch. He says it's as good as done. Something wrong with the books, is there? I'm not sure what, exactly. But with Mr Pinch being in so much trouble, I was determined that the Thurrocks won't be used to give the Captain any excuse. I knew Harry would agree with me, on that. So when the house was empty, excepting Harry and me, I told the truth."

"To Harry?"

"Of course, to Harry."

"What accounts?" asked Peggy.

"Pinch isn't the father of my baby," Edna said.

"I see."

"It isn't possible."

Peggy, smiling, became conscious of having a stupid look on her face. "I see."

"I was already pregnant when Harry asked for your husband's help."

For an age, neither spoke. Peggy collected cups and saucers from her mother's old dresser, and brought in a bottle of milk from the back step. Edna sat down at the table because her legs ached.

"I'm not sure that I understand," said Peggy without pushing for a reply.

"You do," Edna said. "You understand that I'm a trollop. You called me a filthy, filthy woman and I suppose you're right. You won't want me to say what makes me behave the way I do, but when I caught him, Berkeley, laying traps on our land, he suggested and I couldn't stop myself."

Peggy stayed quiet. This wasn't the sort of talk that she wanted to hear in her home but 'things needed to be settled'. She expected worse to come. She found things to do that helped her avoid Edna's face. Now and then, she looked through the window but she couldn't see Six in the back garden. She was sure the woman wasn't listening at the door.

"When I realised I was having a baby, I was in turmoil. I couldn't see what to do. Every trick I thought of would stumble on the same question. No matter what I could say, Harry had no grounds for believing that he was the father. Then, knowing nothing, he proposed seeking help from PC Pinch. Oh God, I thought my prayers had been answered. Honestly, that's just what I thought. I'd done something wrong and here was a sign that I'd been forgiven."

"Indeed," Peggy said quietly, keeping her true thoughts to herself.

"I would have the baby. Everyone would think that Harry was the father. Harry would think Pinch, and Berkeley would be none the wiser."

"Ernest? He's just a boy."

Edna shook her head.

"Very well," said Peggy, hoping the woman would say no more about her frolics with the village lad. "Who else knows?"

"Nobody, I promise. Lady Anne suspected something but she got too clever for herself."

"Tell me."

"When Harry went to the Corquets for help, the Major told Lady Anne that it was bunkum. We didn't need any help, he said, because Boy Berkeley was already giving me a seeing-to. She came across to Thurrocks, on one of Pinch's afternoons, and saw him. She put two and two together and got it wrong. Pinch, not Berkeley, had been seeing to me all along, she thought."

Peggy asked, "Did the Major attempt to blackmail you?"

"Blackmail? No, why would he? If he wanted to threaten someone, he'd have gone to Pinch. Pinch had the most to lose." She sighed, "Even though he had done nothing."

"Done nothing?"

"Oh, I was good and worried when I found out that he couldn't make a job of it. Just once, that's all I needed. You see, he had to believe that he'd seeded me, or he would be left with the question. If not him, who? I begged him to keep trying. How I was cursing him inside my head. 'You soft old goat, just do it to me once and my secret will be safe.' But he never came up to scratch. He told me that he'd had difficulties since Elfrida died. I let him talk about it for hours, but it didn't help"

Peggy faced the window. "Did he talk about our marriage?"

"He didn't have to. I knew you'd be having the same trouble with him."

"So, in the end?"

"In the end, I said it plainly. I was in calf. I thought, both of you, make what you will of it. They were a couple of twerps. Pinch thought Harry. Harry thought Pinch. Everything had come good for me again. Lady Anne thought Pinch was the father, but she'd keep quiet, and Boy Berkeley couldn't have cared less. If only Captain York hadn't started asking questions. I got scared, I suppose. I couldn't keep the truth to myself any longer. I told Harry. But I promised and promised that no-one would find out. He said that we could have trusted Pinch, if he had been the father, but young Berkeley never knew what he was going to say next. The truth was bound to come out, he said, and he couldn't face a village that knew how we had behaved. He went out that morning and he never came back."

Peggy watched WPC Six weeding the flowerbed. She was too big to bend or stoop and, when she knelt, everything looked ready to burst. It's half past twelve, she thought, but Pinch would have the sense to be late for lunch. And after lunch, Peggy was going to check the accounts and registers, page by page. "Well, Pinch and I are fine in all departments of our marriage," she lied, without turning around. At last, she could pretend to have something that the Thurrock woman hadn't. "No problem at all. In fact, I have to slow him down." She couldn't believe that she was talking in this way. She prayed that she wouldn't let herself down by blushing.

The woman said, "Please tell him something from Harry. It's important, to Harry and me."

Peggy said nothing.

131

"The night before he died, Harry was repairing the jetty to our duckpond. I took him some tea and he said he was very sorry that the Black Prince had been stolen, because he always meant Pinch to have it, as a big thank you."

"Edna?" – still with her back to the woman.

"Yes?"

"You can take your puddings home with you."

Peggy heard the woman put her basket in order. She didn't see that Edna was drained white or uncertain on her feet, or that she had to hold onto the kitchen door before venturing any further.

"Edna?" She was determined not to face the woman.

"Yes?"

"I want to know how far things went."

"Nowhere at all. Sometimes ..."

"Do say," she said as primly as a church lady, inviting criticism of her flower arrangement.

"Sometimes," said Edna. "There was just a flicker of life when I spoke about arses."

Peggy shut her eyes tight. That horrible word made everything so much worse. "Ah, yes. He does like to hear about a lady's seat."

Nobody ran for cover, but who wanted to stand in her way or get caught staring? "The fat's in the fire!" drooled the busy postmistress as she shepherded her customers from her shop window. "Best give her a good start. We'll hear all about it before lunchtime." Miss Hestey, gossiping with the crippled char at the Red Lion's side door, tugged the worn overall sleeve. "Oh, her there! She's got the bit between her teeth." There could not have been a better description of Peggy's face. Even Miss Hestey decided to keep to the twitchel and enter the graveyard through a back way.

Peg was at the top of The Street before she realised that she was out of doors with no hat and no handbag, and her shoes were an old pair that she kept for housework. She didn't care. She was in no mood to be ladylike. She didn't care who saw her and what they made of it. Peggy Pinch was in the right, and she wasn't holding back. She hadn't decided what she was going to say to him, except that it would come from the heart and owe nothing to good manners.

She barged through the gate, kicked up the path and shook St Stephen's great door on its hinges.

"Your fault!" she yelled.

The high walls and ceiling batted the words to and fro. The spirits of old craftsmen woke in the roofspace.

"Everything that is wrong with us is because of you!"

Pinch was standing in the aisle, doing nothing.

"How do you think I feel! How do you think I feel!" Her head was bursting with it. "How do you think I feel!" She was so cross that her eyes hurt. "My husband cannot muster," she shouted to the men in the old stone carvings. "And I hear it from the woman I hate more than any other!"

She screamed to the rooftop: "Hate!"

Pinch trod backwards until his heels hit the two steps in front of the pulpit, then he sat down. "Peggy, please. We're in a church."

"Yes, I remember this church." She was marching around the font, her hands waving in the air. "I got married here. I was so proud. Oh, we weren't sweethearts and I knew he didn't love me, but I was marrying the man my mother had chosen. He was safe and strong, and he'd look after me for the rest of my life. He promised! For God's sake, he promised! Folk would look at us, I thought, and say, 'There are the Pinches. Good people, the Pinches.' Well, just hear what they're saying now!"

She marched behind the back pew, gathered a row of hymn books from the shelf and began to throw them in all directions. One, two, three, she counted them in her head. "You made us like this! You and your stupid ghosts in your stupid pudding head." Ten, eleven, twelve. "You talk to Miss C, you listen to Hestey and our priest, you talk to fat Thurrocks in her bed, but you will not talk to your own wife!" Number eighteen knocked a vase of flowers from a windowsill. Peggy liked the sound of it smashing on the floor, so she went to a water jug and, showing off, dropped it on the flagstones.

As she spun round, she fancied the beasts stirred in the faded fresco. Old knights and ladies stared at her from brass memorials, but they could make no difference now. Peggy Pinch had worked up a steam.

The vicar ran in from the vestry.

"I don't care!" Peggy shouted. "I don't care what I'm doing! Get out!" She marched three steps forward. "Get out of your church!"

He swayed a little, looked at Pinch, then turned on his heels and scurried off to his hidey-hole.

"For God's sake, Pinch. How many more women are you going to put between us? You cannot even kiss me – kiss me, Pinch; you can't kiss your wife – because your first one's whispering in your head. She's there, Pinch, between us in our bed. Pinch, she didn't even love you. She couldn't bear to touch you. Pinch wake up!"

She jabbed a finger at him. "You knew! You knew you weren't the father but you let me think it. You let me think that you'd done things with her that you wouldn't do to me. Why? Because you couldn't tell me you were idle." She stood in the middle of the aisle, her feet astride, and dug her hands in her hips. "How could you be so cruel!"

Then she dropped her hands, threw her head back and screamed, "Arse!"

She was standing unsteadily on her toes; they felt the church cellars wanting to rumble beneath her. She drew a deep breath. "Arse!"

Then she shouted it loud and long until her ears tingled and her neck throbbed: "Ar-ar-se!"

She turned her back and left him, wide eyed and open mouthed. She kicked at the broken china as she went from the church.

She was shocked by the gallery of faces overspilling the church-path, men who had interrupted their work, children agog at such criminality, wives who had rushed ill-prepared from their homes, and two mothers with babes-in-arms. Peggy wanted to run, but Miss Hestey grabbed her as she hurried through the porch, and shuffled her through the long, bumpy grass to the blind side of the building.

"Oh, you were good. You were very good." Her face was pointed like a dog's. Her cheeks and lips were jabbering as if they were making three times as many words than came out. "I was there when Widow Redman fired off about the South African War, but

134

she was never half as good as you. Just sit yourself down, Peggy Pinch, and have one of my halves of cigarettes."

They perched on the stone step of an old bricked-up door, where nettles and dock leaves were trying to take over. "I need a hanky," said Peggy. Her throat was sore. "I haven't been crying but all that shouting has made my nose run."

Hestey pulled one from her handbag. "You keep it, Peggy. Seeing you like that was worth ten old handkerchiefs."

"I went too far. I didn't mean to."

"Oh yes you did, and don't go saying you're sorry for it. People will talk about this day for generations. This day in history when one of the village wives went to church and told her copper-husband what a right bugger he was."

"The church is in a mess."

"Now, don't you worry about that. Me and the other women will have that cleaned up in no time. You're our best friend now. If the parson says anything to you, you send him to me. Hestey will soon put him straight. Oh, you were good. Very, very good."

CHAPTER ELEVEN

Three hours later, in the heat of a summer afternoon, the quiet of the Idling Pool was very different from Peggy's row in the church. Pinch hadn't tried to find her, but he had walked slowly through the graveyard and across Thurrock's Top Field so that she couldn't help but see him, if she was looking. He trusted her to follow, once she realised what he was about. After a quarter of a mile, it was clear that they were going to find a place to sit together, but Pinch didn't slow down and Peggy didn't try to catch up. When they reached the Idling Pool, they sat at different edges. Then Pinch stood and surveyed the vale of farmland, as he had done many times since Corquet's murder. He saw the Boy Berkeley, hauling faggots of wood from behind the lineside hut, and Farmer Jones mending a fence on the edge of Thurrock's land. But they were both a long way off. Their figures were miniature and no sound of their work reached up to the Idling Pool.

"These mill plants are lovely," said Peggy. "Try to rake some off for the garden." When she added 'please' she tried to sound a little submissive. That change of tone was the only apology she was going to offer. She was determined that there would be no more small talk; if they spoke, it would be about their marriage.

She watched in silence as he worked. She remembered how, years before their wedding, she had seen him working on the edge of the woods; she had felt the power in every movement of his shoulders. Now, she would say that the strength in his naked back had thrilled her, but she would not have been able to put it into words at the time.

At the Idling Pool, Pinched worked for fifteen minutes, knee deep in the water. "Hestey has given York details of matters that are wrong in our books. I don't know how she knows. How could she? But Corquet's keeper heard him asking her for details of anything we had done wrong, and just now he stopped me, on the way up. He's heard that she's uncovered serious defalcations." He shook his head. "At any other time, I'd say it was all smoke and no fire. But these days, who knows?" Then he climbed onto the bank and started sorting the good plants from the sludge.

She said, "I want to ask some questions because I don't know the answers. If I knew the answers, I wouldn't need to ask the questions."

Pinch worked on. He knew that she was speaking to herself as much as to him. She was explaining her doubts to herself; if they sounded important enough, she would carry on.

"The first time will hurt me, won't it?" she asked.

"I think so, yes," Pinch replied uncertainly. "I don't know much more than you. It hurt Elfrida very much. After the first time, she could hardly bear it." He felt Peggy's eyes on him. "We were together three times. Then she told me that Jessica was there, and we weren't close again. There has been no-one else, Peggy. There are more answers that I don't know, than I do."

They were quiet for a minute. Pinch leaned on his rake and looked at the skyline. "Lovely, up here. When it's quiet in the village, I rest here for an hour or so. I just sit." He held his face to the breeze. "You'd be surprised what wildlife and birds you can hear."

She let his thoughts settle.

She asked, "Would I have to see you?"

Pinch thought it was a curious question, but he wanted to answer as best he could. "I suppose you can close your eyes if we kiss. I think that's natural."

"No. I mean 'see you'. 'You'."

He went back to raking the pond. "You mean, my key to your treasure trove."

The phrase was so un-Pinchlike that Peggy smiled at the sound of it. "Oh, Pinch. That's beautiful," she laughed. (She had nearly called him Pinchie but avoided the mistake in time.)

"I don't know. You could try not to see and I could help. I could try not to show you."

"Only, I've never seen a gentleman's key. Not in grown-ups."

"I should hope not, Mrs Pinch. Whoever would have shown you? There's no ignorance in that."

"And ..." but her voice weakened.

"Ask all you want." He stumbled over his words. "But no more than you want, if you want. Don't fret yourself, Peg-si."

"I suppose I would want to look, just once, to see. Sometime, before we did it. So that I would know."

"Goodness. I can't imagine how we'll arrange that," he said lightly.

"Yes," she confirmed. Then: "I want to see Pinchie's key to Pegsie's treasure trove." It felt as if they were building their own language together.

"But that's not what you were going to ask," he said.

"No. I know."

"You said 'and'."

She felt the colour come to her face. She shook her head. "No, it doesn't matter. Anyway, forget Clemmie's idea. I'm not sitting up in my bed like some painted sacrifice, listening for footsteps of doom on the stairs. In fact, I ... oh God." She sighed, "Of course my God. Oh, heavens. Pinch, how could I be so blind? It's Elfrida's bed. It's Elfrida's bedroom. Oh, Lord, how could we have made it so difficult for ourselves? Right. The bedroom is out of the question, and tomorrow I'll burn the bed in the garden."

Pinch laughed. "I don't think we need to go that far."

"Oh yes, we do. Pinch, there are so many things, like layers of lace curtains, between us. We have to take them down, one by one, layer by layer. We need to be patient, yes, but we can't wait and do nothing. We have to do things. Burning the bed is a good thing to do. I think you should do it with me."

He stood on the bank, pulling the muddy weeds from the rake. "You said it was all my fault. Peg, even when you have pulled away all the curtains, it might still be my fault."

"I know. We're going to be patient, didn't I say? But we do things that help."

He didn't look confident.

"I'm told." (Be damned if she was going to mention Edna Thurrock's name.) "I'm told that talk of sit-upons produces a flicker of life. That might include mine, do you think?"

He was smiling at her. "Why, Mrs Pinch. 'Sit-upon' is such a delicate term for you."

She buried her face. "Oh! Horrors! What made me use that awful word? It's horrible. I hate it. And I shouted it, like a fishwife!"

He sat beside her. "And?"

"And?"

"You said 'and'. You haven't told me what 'and' was."

She peeped through her fingers. "Can't," she said. "Embarrassed. Can't possibly."

CHAPTER TWELVE

When the murders were over and done with, when the third of the three deaths had been absorbed, and the killer had been hung in the county gaol, the village folk said that the last Thursday was the quiet before the storm. They spoke of sunshine that lasted beyond seven o'clock, and a stillness in the trees that made them think of those clammy days when bad news came home from the Great War.

No carts or motorcars trundled down the village street, no-one laboured in the yards or outhouses. There was no sound of shooting in the woods, bells at the church, or playing in the ditches. In the Red Lion the landlady stood at an empty counter. At eight o'clock she decided to scrub the skittle alley; it didn't seem like an evening when gentlemen would want to play skittles. Queen O'Scots was put out at nine. By ten past she was sitting on the roof of Pinch's bicycle shed. (She would still be there at twelve, but there's no telling what she made of the goings-on between. Probably she witnessed more than any other pair of eyes that night.) She heard the Willowby children being called in for supper, and the plodding of Miss Hestey's heavy boots as she wheeled her bicycle up the street. Fresh flowers for the church were packed tightly in the wicker basket on her handlebars.

The postmistress interrupted her, half-way up the lane. "There's talk of cancelling Monday's march, saying it would be disrespectful after two wicked deaths."

"It's been done before," said Hestey. Monday was May Day and the villagers liked to walk down the street, as one, during the evening.

Mrs Porter wanted to say something more. They must have promised to meet later on, because Miss Hestey, in agreement, waved awkwardly over her shoulder as she pressed on, and the mistress went back to her Post Office. But she left the shoplight on and the door ajar.

Miss Carstairs was knitting, content to listen to the heavy ticking of the grand clock. She muttered occasionally, counting her stitches and, after every third row, she paused to look out of the parlour window. "What goes on, Queen O'Scots?" she sighed. "You're out there somewhere, so you must know." She returned her attention to her needles. "Ours is a village with so many secrets," she said. She knew that nothing could be sorted until the scandals were told. They needed to be shown daylight. Matters had gone too far. She shook her head. She was thinking of the vicar's silliness with Lady Anne Corquet. Two days ago, when spiteful Miss Hestey wanted to tell tales to the bishop, Miss Carstairs said that these matters should be kept within the village. But now the couple were almost showing-off. Inspite of their standings, the vicar and Lady Anne seemed to care so little for their village. "Peggy Pinch is right," Miss Carstairs muttered as her needles went click-click-click. "The new habit of shouting across the street won't do. It's a sympton of something more profound and it will not do. We're slipping our stitches, that's what we're doing." The clock chimed the three-quarter hour, and Miss Carstairs wondered if she might treat herself to an extra cup of tea. She never boiled her malt drink before eleven o'clock.

The Pinches were in their sittingroom with an easy silence between them. Something they had rarely savoured before. Pinch divided his time between the complicated jigsaw, leaning forward, and, leaning back, an old bound copy of The Idler's Journal. He liked Hutchinson's drawings. Through the window he saw Steward Orton walk down the street, respectfully taking off his pork pie hat as he passed the War Memorial. Peggy was sitting on the two-seater couch. Ledgers and registers of different colours and sizes sat beside her. She had checked them carefully, but found no deficiencies. Tomorrow she would check the inventories. Now, she was altering a dress.

"Miss Carstairs has given in. She has one of the wirelesses," she said.

"Does she look silly?"

"Yes."

"I can't think it's natural," said Pinch. "Sitting with things in your ears."

Peggy hoped that her husband noticed that she was trying to stitch the dress so that it would sit more provocatively on her behind. If he did – and she was very obvious in what she was doing – she would give him a couple of days, before she tried it on, to think how it might look on her. 'One of my measures in mind,' she called it to herself.

"Do you want one?" he asked.

"Oh, no. As you've always said, they are silly things and they'd get in the way."

He looked up. "Are we the only people in the village who haven't?"

"Oh no," she said. "Only nearly."

WPC Six had gone up for an early night, which was no relief for the Pinches because there was always a threat that she would come downstairs again. While she didn't, she rolled over every twenty minutes, her huge body making the bedstead creak and strain like a giant liner under stress.

"Your phone call to Thurrocks Farm on the night Corquet died? Did you speak to that woman?"

"No, I only spoke to Harry," replied Pinch without looking up. "I don't think she was there."

"Did you mention her name?"

Pinch thought for some minutes. He was leaning over his jigsaw with two or three pieces between his fingers. He fitted a slither of chestnut brown to complete a horse's flank. "Yes. Harry asked me if anyone had told me that Corquet was due out that night, and I said, 'Yes, Edna'."

Peggy tightened her lips at his mention of the woman's name.

"Another thing," she began. "Berkeley didn't see Miss Hestey in Polly's garden. He saw Polly that night – when he had no business to – but he didn't see Hestey."

142

"They could have missed her."

"Suppose she never went there at all."

"Peggy, you've said all this before."

"The wrong affair," she said, loud and clear. She put the dress aside and tucked a nuisance of hair behind her ears. She said it again, nodding to herself with satisfaction.

"Wrong affair?" Pinch asked.

"York suspects that you murdered Corquet because he thinks you're muddling ducks with Edna Thurrocks."

"Muddling ducks?"

"It's Jessica's way of putting it. I called at her cottage and she said it about Lady Anne and the vicar."

"Muddle ducks? Heaven knows what people make of it."

"I know it was my silliness that made the captain suspicious in the first place."

"Look, can we stop this captain nonsense? The man's an inspector and, I suspect, not even a real one of those."

"He heard that I tipped slops over that woman, and he guessed that I was jealous. But suppose, just suppose, that he's got the right idea but the wrong affair. Look, we know that the vicar and Lady Anne are seeing each other. Suppose, just suppose, that they paid Thurrock to get the Major out of the way."

Pinch sniffed. "Flying a bit high."

"It is, Pinch. I know it's the right idea but the wrong affair."

"You forget," he said, sitting back in his armchair, "that the Major was the one handing over the money."

"Smart. A man is tricked into paying for his own murder. So clever."

"But it was me who suggested that the Thurrocks should receive the gift."

"And that put the idea in their heads."

"Good God, Peggity. You're saying a vicar's done a murder."

The front door slammed.

"Pinch, she's gone out."

"She won't be long," he said.

"No. That's the front gate too. She gone out walking."

"She'll be back."

Peggy put her sewing aside. "Pinch, we're going to make love."

He almost choked; just one day ago, his wife would never have said that. "Don't be silly, my dear. She'll be back before you know it."

"We're going to make love and we're not going to do it in the bedroom, where Elfrida will be watching over us." She came to his armchair, knelt down and collected his hands in his lap.

"Peggy, nothing has changed. I won't be any good for you."

"That won't matter," she smiled. "We're going to try, and if we can't, we'll try again another day." She was trying to make her face buoyant and bright. "Go back to Wednesday, to those violent moments before the dreadful Miss Six was dropped into our lives. I was in the kitchen, in tears because you were demanding that I show you my behind, and you were in here, giving me time to prepare. Pinch, we're going to put a happy ending to it. I shall go into the kitchen and wait for you. You, in here. Darling, I want you to think about those stories of me and the vicar. I want you to put the pictures in your head, and when you are ready, rush into the kitchen. I'll be waiting for you." She lifted his hands to her face and kissed his knuckles.

It didn't go according to plan. From the start, he couldn't bring himself to play the fairy-tale of the vicar and the policeman's wife. He tried, but the only pictures that would come to mind were those of that first afternoon when he had been working in the woods. He had been in a sweaty state, with every muscle stretched and every joint exercised to hurting, when he looked up and caught her spying on him. She was in an edge of light, and looked like the mistress of the forest in some medieval myth. For months afterwards, he had thought of her as 'Amber' until he learned her real name.

When he walked into the kitchen Peggy was fully clothed and facing him. Her well covered rear was firmly lodged against the drainingboard. "I can't do it, Pinch! I can do any of it! I can't show you my sit-down. I can't undress in front of you. It's all a sham. I thought I could help you but I can't. You're going to have to do it all, everything; I can't do any of it."

144

He came close to her, made to kiss her but she didn't want it. Then, holding her near, he unpinned her hair so that it fell to her waist, as light and soft as spiders' threads. She weakened, just a little, and he kissed her forehead. Then, lace by lace, button by button, Policeman Pinch undressed his bride.

"It's the pedal cycles." Her voice was tight because she was trying to hold her throat erect as she spoke. "Can't you remember? A year last Hallowe'en, they said that we had to note each lost, found, stolen and recovered pedal cycle in a separate ledger. We received a letter, saying that the logbooks had been distributed to stations but there wasn't enough for us." She was talking quickly. Pinch kept saying 'sssh' and 'quietly now' but Peggy knew that she would collapse if she so much as paused for breath. "Then Sergeant Willis came on a supervisory and made a red entry that we hadn't started a separate pedal cycle register, and we were supposed to make repeated applications, but we never did, Pinch, and now it's nearly two years." Her eyes were fixed on his face. "Please don't look at my body. Please, please, I know I'll die. You won't, will you? Don't look at my body, Pinch. Just my face. Oh, my dear, this is dreadful. They've warned us twice, you see. Two warnings and eighteen months, we've really no excuse. And then, Boxing Day to make matters worse. Don't you remember, the baker's boy had his bicycle stolen last Boxing Day and we're supposed to have registered it in a separate log, and we haven't even got a separate log even though they've told us twice and written it in red in our daily journal ... oh!"

Pinch lifted her off her feet, carried her naked body to the kitchen table, checked that the wooden surface was clear, then sat her on it.

"Oh Pinch. The locomotive. Oh, this is awful, just awful. Oh, no, I know I'm going to die. The model locomotive. I think Miss Six has found it. She was going through the lost property cupboard and says she found it in a box at the back. Oh, truly awful. I want to close my eyes until you've done with me. She wasn't sure, because it was so well hidden and she came to me and I said don't worry and I'm sure it was nothing to do with the murder, I said. Was I right?

Oh God, this is just the worst, worst moment of all my life. I don't know anything. I don't know how I'm supposed to be. I don't know what I'm supposed to do. You'll have to do it all without me. Oh God, I shall faint. I know I will. Oh, why can't I just die? It's too thoroughly awful. There cannot be anything as bad as this. Oh, God, I must be awful for you. Oh God, why can't it be over?"

As Reverend Beamish, wearing an old pair of Pinch's pyjamas trousers, stood at the back bedroom window in Larksteer Cottage and looked across an uncultivated sector of Corquet's estate, he recalled Pinch's prediction that the village would see two distressed sales in a twelvemonth. With Thurrock's death, it seemed inevitable. The vicar and Lady Anne had always accepted that they had no future beyond a secret affair. Now, although they had agreed not to discuss it, he saw that they had a chance, if they were patient, if they behaved moderately, if people thought kindly of them, if ...

Of course, it would become more complicated.

"Don't think of tomorrow," Lady Anne said kindly. She was lying naked on an old, badly repaired bed, with a single linen sheet twisted and screwed around her limbs with pretended recklessness. "Are you watching for Jesse? I said she's sleeping at Manor Farm tonight. No-one can disturb us until morning."

He stayed at the window. "Will you sell?"

"Or will I buy?" she teased. She sighed and lazily kicked her legs. "My brother owns Manor Farm. I have very little say in it."

He turned to face her. "Your brother? You've never mentioned him."

"Because I've never known that you were interested in my money. Come back, darling. To bed." When he didn't move towards her, she explained, "My brother had always said that he would not sell while Eustace was here to manage affairs. Believe me, I'm the one person in this valley who needed to keep the arrogant old goat alive. Don't worry. We can't sell. The proceeds wouldn't cover half the debt. Anyway, we won't hear what he thinks, if the workers play up. My bother is determined to drive lorries out of Liverpool docks. He hopes to get a military escort. That will keep him busy, darling. If there is a strike, I shall go to one of the cities. I shall want to do something."

He didn't respond. He didn't believe that there would be a workers' revolt, or any kind of threat to the constitution. He'd seen no stomach for it in his parish.

He shrugged, and said, "Perhaps the common people will make a better fist of things."

"In the meantime," she laughed. "You must stop Ernest Berkeley telling stories about you chastising sweet Peggy Pinch's derrière. If the villagers believe him, you're for it with the old bish."

"That's Miss Hestey, not Berkeley, and I've got the matter in hand."

"Also, my dear, there's talk of you and Polly the maid."

"Then there ought not to be."

"Did you call on her when she was alone in the house, the night after Eustace died?"

"Yes, and many times before that. I am a vicar; it's part of my duty to call around my parish."

She smiled mischievously. "Like, for instance, Larksteer Cottage?" She sighed, "It's the 'many times before' that people are fussing about,"

The vicar sat on the edge of the lumpy mattress. Lady Anne smiled when she saw that he couldn't resist looking at her wide and floppy breasts. She folded her hands behind her head to make the most of them. "Still, it will stop the peasants talking about you and me."

"I think Pinch was after Eustace's money. He was trying to divert the gift from the church to the Thurrocks, while all the time he was playing chums with the farmer's wife."

"Muddling ducks, darling. We are at Larksteer, remember. We must use thin Jessie's figures of speech." She rolled onto her tummy and shook her hair free. Men liked to see her a little overweight, she thought.

"With Harry Thurrock dead," reasoned the vicar, "and, you tell me, Edna carrying a Pinch-child, he stands to gain much more than he thought."

"Well, he won't get his hands on Thurrock Farm. Jones from Home Farm holds the mortgage."

"Jones has? You've never said."

"No, quite so. I never did say, did I? Now come to me, and stop thinking about murders."

Woman Police Auxiliary, Number Six, was gasping and panting, and rolling her head on her shoulders. She threw her face back so that she could breathe straight through her nose. "The worst thing, I've ever seen," she was trying to say. "Worse than the devil himself." She was on the cusp of running but knew that she would fall over if she did. She was wincing with the pain in her hips and she felt her ankle nearly go as she turned into the garden gate. She shouted out loud, but it was more like a cry than a shout. I'm there, she thought, pushing herself through the front door. "Mr Pinch, come quick," she tried to yell but, because of her gasping and panting, all she did was wail. Then she stood on the edge of the kitchen and screamed.

Peggy was screaming too, so she didn't hear. Peggy was digging her nails into the swollen muscles of his shoulders and deliberately making his broad back carry all of her weight. Her neck was flushed, and the hair on her head glistened, beautifully, with perspiration. "Oh arse, arse, arse!" she cried out as he worked.

Then she saw Six, still screaming, and the two women screamed at each other. Peggy tried to keep her head still so that she could bring the fat woman's face into focus, but Pinch gave her no chance of that.

"Stop, now. No, stop."

Instead of thrashing in ecstasy, Peggy was trying to fight her husband off, but Pinch didn't realise.

Six walked backwards and collapsed in a pile on the parlour carpet. Peggy sent Pinch, with his bundle of clothes, to the back garden and was still drawing her dress over her head when she got to the sobbing woman. "I'm sorry, Six. We're both so sorry."

"No, no. It's not you. It's Miss Hestey in the church. They've put her head in the iron mask. She's dead."

CHAPTER THIRTEEN

The villagers came out of their houses. Carstairs and the Pinches. The postmistress and her brother. The labourers from Back Lane. Husbands who had left their wives indoors. Wives who had browbeaten their men into coming. Widows and widowers who lived in old cottages. Some rougher types, who often walked at night and had the foresight to bring lanterns. (They knew that modern torches would be no good for a job like this.) Children appeared at bedroom windows. "Where's the vicar?" some people wanted to know. "He's not been seen yet." Well mannered dogs were kept inside, but the strays and mongrels joined the troop as it trod up the village street. The downtrodden of Wretched Lane waited for the hubbub to die down, then they crossed the churchyard, quiet and unseen.

Peggy and Pinch weren't in the church before the bell began to toll. At this time of night, its signal could be nothing but a call for the community to gather in dreadful circumstances. (Later, Meggastones, the verger, said that ringing the church bell was his best way of summoning the vicar to his duties. That seemed nonsense; there would have been more discreet ways of doing it. While some insisted that the soulful bellringing was part of Meggstones' theatre, those at the heart of the village knew that it was the old man's way of expressing sorrow, despair and a need for people to come together.)

Miss Hestey had been propped, like a fractured doll, against the stone wall. Chips and dust, from the holes where the fixings had been, had fallen on her shoulders and into her hair. The medieval bridle had been forced around her head, and the iron tongue jabbed into her disfigured mouth. Her coat and dress were torn, her legs stuck out at hideous angles below their knees. Her eyes bulged. Each person who looked wanted to know if the torture had been inflicted on her before she died; some stood transfixed, others looked around for clues. Everyone looked at her bulging eyes.

Pinch took charge. "Someone get a decent cloth and cover her. There must be a robe in the vestry. Verger!"

He noticed that some people had turned away from the body; they filled two rows of pews and were praying, led (and comforted) by Muriel Moorcroft's rich local accent. "There must be fifty people in here," he whispered to Peggy. "Where the hell is the vicar?"

"Pinch, please. We're in a church."

Three men had found a grubby cassock, with an old dribble of jam down its front, and were ready to cover Miss Hestey.

"Yes, yes. Please go ahead," Pinch told them.

Peggy lifted herself onto her toes and said, "Pinch, I know who did this."

"Then you must keep it to yourself. I won't allow you to put yourself in danger, Peggy. The man who did this is capable of far worse, if he's cornered."

"Pinch, we have to put a stop to it."

"No. You will say nothing."

Farmer Jones intruded on their whispered conversation. "Can I help, Pinch? Me and two strong fellows, do you think? Your place is in here with your people."

"Where's the vicar?" Pinch asked again.

"At Larksteer, I'm afraid," said the farmer. "He'll know nothing of this."

Then Captain York was at St Stephen's great oak door, his short figure silhouetted in the moonlight. He wore motorcycle boots and gauntlets and a huge macintosh. The macintosh was open and billowed behind him, giving him a supernatural look. Did the man see himself as an avenging angel or the witchfinder general? In that church, where the previous twenty minutes had conjured up a great coming-together, the King's Army Officer at the door was an outsider. No-one wanted him in.

Pinch coughed politely.

"I have come to see Miss Hestey," York announced, and the congregation fell silent.

Pinch stepped forward. "She is dead. She has been strangled and her face disfigured by the ancient scold's bridle."

York's slow, even footsteps echoed from the stone floor. His face was grave and, as he walked to the centre of the church, his eyes didn't release the village constable. Every one could see that he despised Pinch.

"Miss Hestey telephoned the Divisional Police Station this evening. Her message was relayed to me. She said that she had important information about your conduct which she promised to deliver into my hand at this church at ten o'clock. I have come here and I find that Miss Hestey has been murdered before that evidence can be given up."

"Pinch, you can't let this happen," Peggy whispered, but loud enough for others to hear.

"Constable Pinch, I took the precaution of asking Sergeant Willis to follow me in the Police Oxford, so that you can be taken into custody."

Peggy grasped her husband's elbow. "You must speak up!"

"There is ample evidence of your involvement in two murders in this parish."

It's the end, thought Pinch. He knew that he couldn't be convicted of any murder, but the prosecutor would bolster the case with stories of Pinch's wrongdoing in the village. The goings-on with Edna Thurrock in her loft. The bullying of his wife. Intrigues with Reverend Beamish and Major Corquet (that would include an intimation of corruption if not blackmail). They might even try to make something of his early morning breakfasts with the gamekeeper and the steward of Home Farm. 'I'm sacked.' Although he couldn't put a finger on it, he sensed a future, wandering alone through a succession of miserable circumstances. The loneliness, he could not argue with. That was his own doing. But he hoped that more people would see him as a fool, not a scoundrel.

"What is your case?" he demanded.

Captain York was ready to take hold of his arm. "Don't make a fight of this, Mr Pinch."

"No!" The postmistress stepped forward. "I have the letter that Miss Hestey promised to give you, on behalf of us all." She was holding six sheets of best bond paper, tied with ribbon like an Edinburgh lawyer's brief. "We have all signed the testimonial, saying that the Pinches are good people. We will allow no other couple to occupy our Police House. Peggy was born in the village and went to our little school. No-one hereabouts will forget the fortitude with which she faced the death of her parents. If she has been loyal to Pinch in difficult times, we all know that is because she judges him to be a good man and an honourable husband. That, alone, would be enough. But each one of us has seen the work that this man has done since coming to our village, twelve years ago. Our Timothy Redman, our young policeman, had been sent to France and Pinch arrived with the news that he would not be coming back. You can't understand, Mr York, Tim's death seemed to bring all our soldiers' deaths into one, and Pinch led us through that sorrow. He did so quietly, in his own way, and knowing his place. Knowing his place, Mr York, was important. He isn't above us, this man. We trust his simple ways, but his wisdom isn't like the judgments of a prejudiced grandfather. He steps back and lets the village go on its way. But his promise is that we shall always see him. He is there on patrol or standing at the War Memorial, or sitting with Boy Berkeley or, so sad to say, Miss Hestey on our village green."

York had heard enough. "All that's as maybe, but we are talking here of two murders."

Someone coughed.

Polly Gunn, who had been unnoticed and was too small to be seen above other shoulders, pushed her way to the front. "I've seen him with his trousers and pants down. I have. I did." She was twitching. She tied her fingers in knots and her toes were trying to kiss one another. "I was walking through Middle Thicket and I saw PC Pinch sitting by the Idling Pool and had nothing on, except his shirt." She nodded quickly, like a pecking hen.

"Polly Gunn! How dare you bark such a spiteful lie!" cried Mrs Porter, grabbing the accuser's shoulders.

"You want to watch your tongue, my girl!" demanded Jasmine Moorcroft. "Was anyone with you?"

Polly bit her lip. "Well, no. I can't say who, can I?" She looked from face to face. She wished that she hadn't spoken up. Always, leave things to other people. That's what her mother had told her.

"So, you've no witness to join you in your wicked lie?"

"Please, Mr Pinch?"

Pinch stepped back. "We really shouldn't go making things up, Polly. Now, off you go and we'll say no more about it.

But Porter gripped the girl's shoulder and push her up the aisle. "There, Mr Pinch is prepared to let you off. Well, not so fast. If I were you, Polly Gunn, I'd be thinking of getting my scandalous self out of trouble. I shall be seeing your mother about this. Mark my words."

"She tells the same lies about our vicar," someone called out.

"Or similar," shouted another. "Very, very similar."

Polly was crying loudly now.

"And she says Farmer Jones isn't as he should be!"

"And Miss Hestey! She said the same about her."

"Now, just a minute," began the captain

But Moorcroft stepped in front of him. "She's not said anything, Captain. She's not said anything that she's not taken back."

Porter had dragged the victim to a square of rough paving at the edge of the nave. "You kneel there! You pray to be forgiven. None of your blubbering, girl. We want to hear you plead that you're evil tongue be ripped from your mouth."

The girl's face was soaked in tears.

"Enough!" bellowed Captain York. "I have come to arrest a man for murder."

"Murders that I can solve fairly," said Peggy, "if you will allow me a few private words."

The little captain was in a fix. He couldn't allow Peggy to make accusations of murder in front of an audience. Who knows what trouble that might bring? Yet, if he walked outside with her, he was sure that Pinch would get away. And York was determined to make a prisoner of this disreputable policeman.

Meggastones, sitting on a ancient but sturdy bench that was accustomed to bearing the plump verger's weight, read the captain's mind. "Oh, don't you go worrying about an escape, sir. While Pinch is in our church, he has sanctuary against any arrest."

What nonsense.

York studied the old man's craggy face. "That's mumbo-jumbo. The laws of sanctuary are long gone."

"An old rector's note in our parish chest says contrary. A signed certificate, I'd say it is." He leaned forward. "A charter!"

"Even then. Even if. Sanctuary has to be claimed," York argued uncertainly. "Are you claiming sanctuary, Pinch?"

Meggastones piped up, "Doesn't have to. It's well known that if a fugitive has lost his mind, the villagers can claim sanctuary on his behalf. Me? I've always said the Pinch was a little mad." He turned to his neighbours. "What do you say?"

Everyone could hear Polly sobbing in the corner of the church. She rubbed her face, pulled at her hair and tugged at her uncomfortable clothing. Oh, she was praying, that was certain, but no-one could make out her garbled entreaties. Mrs Porter gave her ferocious looks; she wanted to give the girl another dose of the medicine.

"Do we say that Pinch stays here?" Mr Meggastones called at the top of his voice.

York protested. "This is rubbish!" But York was a military man, not a police superintendent, and his knowledge of the law was scant.

"Well, people who say it's true are here," Meggastones said in a country drawl. "And people who say it isn't are somewhere else. That as good as finishes it, don't you think?"

"Are you claiming sanctuary, Mr Pinch?" York repeated.

Meggastones wouldn't be kept quiet. "While we wait, Miss Hestey's soul suffers in purgatory. She cannot rest until her body is properly treated."

No-one had noticed Sergeant Willis enter the building. He was a diffident man who looked ready to sink into himself. He wore the black tunic and peaked cap of a uniformed driver which, along with his modest bearing, made him look more like a chauffeur than a police sergeant.

"Sir," he began moderately. "I have been handed news by a motorcycle dispatch rider. A notice to all police posts that I am required to tell you straightaway."

The church went quiet and all eyes were on him.

"Yes, yes. What is it?" snapped his captain.

"A national coal strike has commenced. The trades union council is declaring a General Strike at twelve hours notice. Trouble has been reported at the presses of the Daily Mail and Morning Post. Sir, the emergency is on."

York's anger was bitter. "Pinch! Are you claiming sanctuary!"

"No-one need claim anything, if only you'll listen to me," said Peggy calmly. She had already taken his arm but he resisted, so wedded was he to the idea of arresting Pinch.

Then Polly came running through the church, demanding, "Mr Pinch, tell the truth."

Pinch nodded. "The truth is," he began.

Peggy jumped between them. "The truth is, Polly Gunn, that you murdered Major Corquet, then you murdered Miss Hestey to keep her quiet."

"You!" she yelled and leapt at Pinch.

She was such a light figure that he threw her off by turning his shoulder. But she landed on her feet and came at him again, spitting and scratching at his face.

"Get back, Pinch!" he heard someone shout.

When Mrs Porter and Miss Moorcroft braced the girl between them, she screamed like a child in a tantrum, slapping her feet on the ground, tossing her head, wrenching her arms so that they hurt in the women's grip. "You're all sinners!" she shouted.

"Take her to the ground," Mrs Porter said spitefully. She twisted the girl's hair in her fingers and pulled her down.

"Where's our vicar and the Major's lady!" Polly shouted, kicking wildly and thrusting her shoulders this way and that, trying to roll over.

Miss Moorcroft had blood on her face and forearms. Mrs Porter was jerking her head backwards; she was sure the girl had damaged her nose.

"They can't be here because they're sinning!" Polly cried. "Just like you at Farmer Thurrocks."

At first, Pinch was sure that no-one realised she was accusing him. Then Miss Carstairs quietly told him to keep out of the way. "You're making things worse for her, Pinch."

Two other women were on their knees, trying to lock Polly's legs. Moorcroft twisted her hair some more, sure that the pain would shut the girl up, and Mrs Porter was digging her knees into Polly's side.

York stepped forward. "Now, enough there. Enough"

But Verger Meggastones put himself in the captain's way. "Best, you leave this to us. We know how to quell a loose-tongued woman."

"She's a minx!" shouted a voice at the back.

"A minx!"

"I heard you telling him," Polly shouted. "Deny it! Say it's not true! Tell lies and fibs. Deny it, you said. Peggy Pinch is a liar."

But, once again, only Miss Carstairs seemed to make sense of it. "Take the captain outside, Peggy. Explain to him how Polly did the murders."

York might have thought that it was his duty to stay but, as Peggy encouraged him from the church, he looked like a man who was relieved to be led away. "That was nonsense," he was saying to the last. "All that talk of sanctuary."

"You're all sinners!"

Now, the villagers moved in. Each wanted to be close enough to reach for her hair or kick her.

"Keep the little rat quiet!" someone called out.

Another: "Don't let her speak!"

Polly looked straight at Miss Carstairs. "Where d'you get all your things? From the schoolhouse, didn't you, and everyone said they'd let you. Go ahead and steal, that's what they said. Thieves and sinners. Thieves and sinners. But none for mother and me."

156

Moorcroft twisted Polly's ankle. The girl screamed.

"All done in secret. In the keeper's cottage and the back of the post office." She sobbed, "All done after hours, when you think that God's not watching."

Meggastones had wrapped his weighty arms around the girl's legs. "We'll get her out to the police car," he said to Jones, who had taken charge of her shoulders.

"Where's the Prince!" she shouted. "You've been stealing the Black Prince. First, you. Then, him. Thieves. That's what you are. Where is it now?"

Then Berkeley ran into the church. "No!"

"Ernest didn't know," Polly cried as the two big men lifted her from the floor. "No, you can't take me. Not without my mother. She's in Bolton. Mother's in Bolton."

"This isn't right," pleaded Berkeley, in tears.

Pinch took the youth's arm and gently guided him aside. "Leave this to Sergeant Willis," he said.

But Sergeant Willis had his hands full. People were everywhere. Some went ahead and opened the door of the police car. Some cleared the path of stones and any obstacle. Some trotted alongside Meggastones and Jones, ready to grab the girl if she struggled too hard.

"I never knew as for sure," Berkeley said quietly. He was sitting with Pinch at the bottom of the staircase to the bell-tower. "I guessed enough not to ask her any questions. You see, that night, she was sure that Corkers was going to tell Thurrock that I had been misbehaving with Mrs Edna. Farmer Harry would have surely come after me then. With his gun, more's the likely. Polly didn't know any way of stopping that, other than shooting Corkers before he caused the trouble."

"Captain York, let us stick to matters we are sure of," Peggy said, as the black patrol car moved down the village street.

They could hear Pinch telling the congregation that he had no report of civil insurrection, so far, but it would be better if they all went to their homes.

"Pinch's telephone call to the Thurrocks was always going to be the crucial part of your enquiries. You recognised that, I know, from the moment you came to our home. But you didn't understand why, did you? Oh, it had me puzzled too. Until Polly Gunn told me that Pinch was talking to that woman instead of her husband."

"He spoke to Mrs Thurrock? But the farmer told me his wife wasn't at home that evening."

"No, she wasn't," Peggy agreed. "But that wasn't important, was it?"

"Wasn't it?"

"But Polly thought she was because Pinch said, 'Yes, Edna.'"

"And that made it important?"

"Oh, crucial."

As they walked down the middle of the lane, Queen O'Scots stepped out from the verge and walked between them. It was as if she had identifed the murderer from the start and deserved to be there at the denouement.

"Although Polly misunderstood the conversation, it tells us that she was close enough to hear the words. Once we understand that, all we have to do is place each fact in order."

"I see," said the captain, taking this lesson in policework with graceful, but not untroubled, humility.

"And then there is the clue of Carstairs' cat."

"That's important, too?"

"Oh, just as crucial."

"Mrs Pinch, can you start at the beginning?"

Behind them, people were already drifting away from the church. No-one was talking and they walked in a shuffle. To many it seemed wrong that a community should walk away from their church without their vicar's blessing, but Reverend Beamish was nowhere to be seen. Then came the sounds of houses being shut up for the night, gates being tied back, boots being beaten. Somewhere, a child was being soothed. Peggy and York saw a light in the back porch of the Red Lion; the landlady had opened up, after hours, for any of her regulars who wanted to talk before putting the day to bed. A horse and cart came into the village from the rough end of

Wretched Lane; it hadn't been summoned but Steward Orton knew that it would be needed to take the body away.

"For years," said Peggy, "stories had blamed Major Corquet for the death of a young soldier in France. Tom Hall told the tale at every opportunity but no-one believed it was true. Then our vicar went to a church conference and heard that the Major might have been guilty, after all. Corquet's response was predictable. He offered money to buy the vicar's silence. But the vicar was having none of it and sought Pinch's advice."

York nodded. "And Pinch said that the Thurrocks were in queer street, and if Corquet wanted to part with his money, Harry and Edna would give it a good home."

"You knew?"

"Harry Thurrock told me, the morning he died."

"But Corquet had other enemies, including Polly Gunn. She despised him for trying to suggest that Boy Berkeley was cavorting with Mrs Thurrock."

"Which he was."

"I am not here to discuss village matters, Captain. However, I do tell you that my husband was not."

"Mrs Thurrock has already corrected me on that point, Mrs Pinch."

"Then that, at least, is one charge PC Pinch is free of."

"Please," York prompted. "The night of Corquet's death?"

"My husband phoned Harry Thurrock to arrange a meeting with Major Corquet at Holt's Crossing. Polly Gunn overheard the conversation. She stole the shotgun from the keeper's den and lay in wait by the railway track. Meanwhile, Miss Hestey was calling for her, and Boy Berkeley did too, later on. When Ernest saw that she wasn't at home, he feared the worst and tried to cover for her, telling the vicar and myself that he'd been with her that night. Later, he recovered the gun from the railway hut and hid it somewhere. I don't think we shall ever find it. Polly felt safe, at first. She could count on Ernest to keep quiet, but when I told her the story of Miss Hestey and Queen O'Scots, she decided that she had to murder the poor woman to keep her quiet."

159

"So, I was mistaken about Mrs Thurrock and your husband. What about the vicar and Lady Anne?"

"We're not gossiping, Captain."

"Or, yourself and the postmistress's brother."

Peggy was outraged. She'd never so much as looked at the man. "That's vicious, Captain York! I can't imagine who has given you such a story. There is no truth in it and I'll thank you not to repeat it. Why, you think you can go round, slandering people with no hesitation."

The captain was content with her reaction; it told him so much. "I'm sorry. I have seen how this village turns on those who speak out of turn," he remarked.

"Yes, well," Peggy said shortly, still cross with him.

He had left his motorcycle at Pinch's garden gate. Peggy invited him indoors, in clipped terms, but he insisted on returning at once to the Divisional Police Station, so that he could interrogate Polly, as soon as she arrived. He said, putting on his fleece-lined gauntlets, "I do apologise, Mrs Pinch. I was quite, quite wrong to indulge in tittle-tattle. I might say that you are a very remarkable lady, Mrs Pinch. Goodnight."

"Before you go, Captain. Did Miss Hestey tell you that something was wrong with my record keeping?"

"Your record keeping?"

"Captain York, you know very well that I keep all the records and accounts in the Police House."

He smiled. "She said that Pinch wasn't exercising proper care in the cell register. She said, people were being locked in there at night, and no record kept. It was a simple matter to check. I looked at the impress for victuals, and found no discrepancy."

"Thank you, Captain. Goodbye."

He kicked the motorcycle engine into life, looked over his shoulder and drew away from the verge. 'I made it up about the postmistress's brother,' he thought as he opened the throttle and roared through the village, not caring now who he disturbed or what they thought of him. 'But her reaction told me that I had been right, two out of three.'

Peggy stood at her gate and watched the motorcycle's tail-light flicker and disappear. Queen O'Scots clawed at the chicken-wire and, when she had made a comfortable bed in the hedgerow, crouched down and watched for new things to interest her. "Your mistress has put her bedside lamp out, Queenie," said Peggy. "You be quiet when you go in, do you hear?" She knew that Pinch would be busy for another hour – he'd want to be sure that everyone was safely home – but she decided to wait for him at the front gate. Tonight, of all nights, she wouldn't be able to settle until he was indoors.

CHAPTER FOURTEEN

Heavy snow fell on Boxing Day and stayed on the ground for two weeks. On the 27th Pinch mustered a labour gang and they shovelled footpaths from the top of the village to the bottom but it was another forty-eight hours before the farm horses could be brought through to clear the ways to the more remote homes in the parish. The trees in Wretched Lane had well protected the cottages so this place became the headquarters for the work. Here, tools were collected, hot meals were carried in and the teams of frozen diggers came back for a warm. The new vicar said it was all right to open Polly Gunn's cottage. At first, the team encroached no further than the kitchen and the back yard but gradually the front room and the staircase and even the two bedrooms were brought into service.

The cottage had been promised to newlyweds in the Spring. The church estates office was grumbling about no rent for the greater part of a year and the new vicar had earned some early respect by championing the young couple's case, although some people thought it was wrong to hurry things until old Mrs Gunn had been allowed an opportunity to collect anything that might be her property.

But Mrs Gunn had not been heard of since the outrage at Holt's Crossing. The villagers had expected to see her within days of Polly's arrest (and two of the women had been chosen to look after her) but days turned into weeks and, by August, people began to speak as if Mrs Gunn wouldn't be coming back. Muriel Moorcroft thought that this had been the woman's intention all along. She'd gone to Bolton, not to look after her wounded father, but because she wanted to be free of Polly for good. The parishioners didn't like that idea; it turned Polly into an abandoned child and cast an uncomfortable light on the way she had been treated.

"The lad won't be back," Miss Carstairs said when she and Peggy were producing hot food in Polly's kitchen. No-one had seen Boy Berkeley since the July evening when, sitting by the memorial with a pint that he had brought across from The Red Lion, he had explained to Peggy that he was running away to work in the dockyards. "No, he won't be back what with Edna Thurrock's time drawing near," the schoolma'am insisted. Peggy gave her a strange look; it was a convention that, just a few days before Edna's time, no-one would allow even a hint that Harry might not have been the father.

"I know," apologised Miss Carstairs. "I know, I know."

Mr Jones of Home Farm had taken over Thurrocks. While no mention of marriage had been heard, his promise that Edna and the child could live in the farmhouse for as long as they liked suggested that there might be grounds later on.

Strange to say, Peggy thought that Edna had faced so many revelations with dignity. The evidence of the trial left no doubt that she and Berkeley had 'muddled their ducks' in the barn loft – only once, but enough – but Edna kept her arrangements with Pinch secret.

The vicar and Anne Corquet were properly shamed. Almost overnight, people had stopped referring to her as 'Lady Anne', (a title to which, Tom Hall reminded them, she had no right) and started to talk of 'the Corquet woman'. The vicar moved to a living in another county.

"And what about you, Peggy Pinch?" Miss Carstairs said as they worked in the kitchen. "Everyone thinks you are a first class detective and I've no doubt that you've been 'consulted'."

"Mrs Henry's vagrant knitting satchel, you mean? It was under her Albert's motorcar cushion." Peggy checked that they were alone in the kitchen, then confided in a whisper, "But Mr Henry was to blame. I talked him into a 'straight cough'. Sshh, I'm sworn to secrecy, Miss Carstairs."

"And who left the Post Office gate open?"

"A mystery unsolved, I'm afraid."

Their discussion was interrupted by chattering and exaggerated exclamations. The postmistress and Mrs Willowby were having a good gossip in the next room.

"Really," said Peggy, with a little extra colour in her cheeks. "They are talking much too loud."

Pinch sent everyone home at four. It was going to be a bitter night and he wanted no-one out of doors after tea. He and Peggy stayed in Polly's kitchen for another three quarters of an hour. By the time they locked up, the dark was drawing in and the broken snow was beginning to freeze again.

"Did you hear them say it?" she shouted, as they manoeuvred a sledge, loaded with two empty tea urns, into the middle of The Street and, inch by inch, got the thing moving.

Pinch called back. "I did, and I saw you looking to see if I'd picked it up." Then: "We're going to have to lean sideways on this thing and push at the same time."

Neither mentioned the freezing cold on their faces.

"Miss Carstairs has promised to bring some soup across, for me to heat on the stove," she said. "I offered her some potato cakes but she wouldn't hear of it."

"Maybe, Peggy love, if you take the rope at the front while I put my weight on the back. God, this wind's getting biting."

It had taken them twenty minutes to get this far, and they were soaked.

"I hope you'll find time to use your Christmas presents this evening," she shouted. "We can't go upstairs until the last. We need to be properly warmed through." She had bought him a set of fine painting brushes, so that he could dust and touch up the Black Prince. It had pride of place these days where the old photographs used to be.

"Come on, Peg," he urged.

"Yes. Together, we can do it."

Slewing this was and that, they passed the Post Office, and Muriel Moorcroft's cottage. At the Willowby house, the children, wrapped in a pair of curtains, were watching from the parlour window.

The sledge had stalled in a rut. "We'll have to leave it here until morning," shouted Peggy. "It's the wind, Pinch, that's so freezing."

They stopped struggling and looked at each other.

Pinch repeated at the top of his voice. "They said,'Mr and Mrs Pinch have worked hard for us today.' I heard them say it, Mrs Porter and Willowby, and loud enough for you to hear, 'The Pinches are good people.'"